Murder on the Backswing

The Mag and Clara Balefire Mysteries

BOOK TWO

REGINA WELLING
ERIN LYNN

Murder on the Backswing

ISBN- 978-1-953044-09-9

Cover design by: L. Vryhof

Interior design by: L. Vryhof

http://reginawelling.com

http://erinlynnwrites.com

First Edition

Printed in the U.S.A.

Contents

Chapter One

"Unbelievable," Margaret Balefire muttered as she raised a pair of magically-enhanced high-resolution binoculars to her eyes and studied something across the street. Her sister, Clara, wondered how she could see anything at all, eyelids narrowed to slits as they were.

"What now? Is Mrs. Green not picking up after her Corgi again?" Mag tended to take the *watch* half of the term *neighborhood watch* to the extreme, even though she'd never be caught dead joining such an organization. In fact, the only group to which she deigned to claim membership was the local witch's coven—and even then, Mag participated only grudgingly.

She cocked her head toward Clara and directed a glare in her sister's direction. "No, Miss Smarty Pants, it's Taylor Dean, that mailman of ours. He just put Georgia Macomb's package under the rain gutter, and it's pouring outside. Yesterday he left our mailbox door open and the check for that console table I sold last week got completely soaked. I had to use a drying charm, and it was still wrinkled so badly the bank cashier gave me a dirty look."

"Are you sure the look was about the check or the fact that you like to bring her half the morning deposit in quarters? I know you think I'm too uptight about using magic for personal gain, but doesn't irritating the teller count as mischief?" Clara shot back.

"It counts as entertainment, Mag said, adjusting the binoculars, "which is in short supply around here. Stop being such a downer."

Clara raised one eyebrow at the statement and opened her mouth for a rebuttal, but the bell tinkled above the door of the shop, signaling the entrance of a customer.

Clara turned her attention to the new arrival and offered the harried-looking middle-aged woman a welcoming smile. "Welcome to Balms and Bygones. I'm Clara, how can I help you?"

"Angela Sinclair," the woman nodded, looking around. "Nice to meet you. I hear you carry the best anti-aging face cream this side of Port Harbor. That true?" The customer, who Clara only vaguely recognized, looked skeptical as she took in the contents of the shop. Since moving to Harmony and opening the store a few months prior, Mag and Clara had been asked why they'd chosen to peddle the odd combination of botanicals and antiques at least a hundred times—basically, by just about every person in town.

Clara shrugged off the unspoken insult and instead forced the corners of her lips into an even deeper smile, "You've heard correctly; I make all the products myself, with locally-sourced ingredients. And my mother,

Margaret, deals in antiques. We can sell you a beauty arsenal, plus a cupboard to keep it all in."

Proving true the adage that whatever a witch sends out into the world comes back to her threefold, Angela Sinclair caught Clara's infectious good mood and cracked an answering grin. "I'm not in the market for furniture, but show me what you've got that can help with these crow's feet."

While Clara peddled her wares, Mag returned her attention to the street where the mailman had delivered three more batches of letters without seeming to care whether they'd made it to the addressees intact. Cursing under her breath, she watched as he ambled down the front walkway and bypassed the "open" sign on the shop door. Without bothering to knock or ring the bell, Taylor deposited a package on the front stoop and continued down the block, not caring that it was raining.

"Rat bastard!" Mag exclaimed, causing Clara and Angela to whip their heads in her direction.

"I don't know how that man keeps his job. I can't have been the only one to notice he's completely incompetent." She griped.

Clara shot daggers at Mag and attempted to usher Angela to the other end of the store, "I'm sorry about my mother. She takes mail delivery very seriously—a sign of her advanced age, I think."

Angela laughed and brushed Clara's apology aside, "Just one of the perks of small-town life. She's not wrong, but you won't get anywhere trying to get Taylor fired. The last time someone quit, it took six months to find a replacement. No one wants the job."

"Wonderful." Mag muttered as she stomped out through the door to retrieve the bundle. She glanced around, did a quick sweep to make sure no prying eyes would witness what she was about to do, and directed a bolt of magic across the street. Mrs. Macomb's package lifted in the air, spun around, and shot onto the dry, covered porch. "You're welcome."

She contemplated tossing another spell toward the mail truck Taylor had left parked at the corner, considering a wet seat fitting punishment for his crime. However, she made the mature decision to refrain, figuring he'd reap what he had sowed eventually, without her interference.

Clara and Angela were chatting like old friends by the time Mag returned to the shop interior.

"The garden club meets on Tuesdays at ten a.m. in the library solarium. Then we fan out to take care of the community plots. Actually, there's a special session tomorrow to discuss how we can battle this hummingbird problem. Have you noticed how much larger they are this year? Maude Prescott was attacked by one when she didn't fill their feeder fast enough, and now her flower beds are full of weeds because she refuses to go into her backyard."

Mag snorted loudly and rudely enough to earn a glare from her sister, which she duly ignored while pretending to dust an antique canning cupboard.

"We have a delivery scheduled for the morning, unfortunately," Clara said with just the right amount of disappointment in her tone. She finished up with Angela, agreed to attend the next regular garden club meeting, and ushered her new friend to the door before descending upon Mag with a furious expression.

"Are you trying to alienate every paying customer who walks through the door?"

"Of course not," Mag said, wrinkling her nose, "and don't talk to your *mother* like that." Though she claimed she wasn't bothered that her outer appearance didn't reflect just how close they were in age, Clara knew it rankled just the same.

"You know, I feel the same way you do, but in the opposite direction. At least you're perceived as the wise old woman you are, whereas I don't look like I've had time to contemplate a midlife crisis—of which I've experienced several."

With only a handful of years between them and, thanks to the blessing of long life bestowed upon all witches, neither of them appeared their actual age— which had already surpassed two centuries. Humans tended to assume Mag was closing in on her eighties and pegged Clara for about fifty years younger. Not even the town drunk would have believed them sisters.

Though she would never mention it to Mag, who wore her battle scars proudly, Clara had been working her way through an obscure collection of magical texts to see if there was a way to reverse the damage done by the Raythe attack that had leached away Mag's youthful appearance.

Mag would give birth to a pink unicorn with a rainbow cottontail if she suspected for one minute her front of indifference had been penetrated. And Clara would do anything in her power to restore what her sister had lost.

A commotion outside caught Clara's attention as she arranged a new batch of lavender pillow spray on a recently-acquired hutch near one of the front windows.

"Maggie, it looks like your mailman is getting his just desserts." Clara waved her sister over.

Taylor had just returned from his trek up and down the waterlogged Mystic Street when Leonard Wayland, half of the couple who owned the house next door to Georgia Macomb, descended his porch steps. Leonard approached the mailman with an angry expression, and Mag bustled outside just in time to hear him spit vim and vinegar.

"I won't stand for this any longer!" Leonard said, waving his mail. "I'll file another complaint with your supervisor if I have to. How difficult is it to close the mailbox door? If my wife's magazines keep getting soaked, I'll either have your job or your head, Taylor Dean!" Leonard shouted, his patience having reached the breaking point.

Taylor took a step back, puffed out his chest, and when he spoke it was too low for Mag to overhear. Whatever he said turned Leonard's face even redder than before and slackened his chin in surprise. Not for long, though, because after a second, Leonard's eyes narrowed and his posture changed to match Taylor's.

"Don't mess with me; I'm a big old man." Mag muttered her own mocking version of the conversation. *"I'm bigger and hairier, too/"* She hmphed. "Idiots, the pair of them."

The discussion petered out quickly, and it didn't look to her like either side had come away entirely happy.

His face devoid of expression, Taylor strolled toward Mag, who stepped into his path. When she lifted her hand, first and middle fingers in a V shape and used it in the swiveling gesture pointing to his eyes and then to hers to indicate he'd better listen, Taylor's eyebrows shot up. And so did Mag's temper.

Mayor Norm McCreery chose that inconvenient moment to appear on the sidewalk, headed toward Balms and Bygones to stare at Clara, Mag could only assume. And so, he was on the spot to hear her grit out the warning, "I'm watching you." A chill fell, one that had nothing to do with the rainy day, and for a split second, something untamed and powerful rose in the old woman's eyes.

Taylor shrugged past her and only turned once to find her gaze still heavy on him as he made for his truck and drove away.

"Problem?" Norm asked.

"Not for long," Mag answered, turning to go back in the shop.

Chapter Two

Beads of perspiration pearled on her forehead, beginning a slow trickle into Clara's eyes by the time Mag bustled into the alchemy lab tucked behind the shop's display floor with a tray full of finger sandwiches and iced tea.

"One of the perks of living in such a small town is that we can take a break for lunch and nobody bats an eyelash," Mag said as she eyed the food. "Heck, even the post office closes down between noon and two o'clock. Want to take a quick walk down the back trail once we've eaten? That big patch of sage needs to be clipped and layered."

Clara wiped her brow, twisted her chestnut mane into a topknot, and secured it with a pencil while, at her command, the bubbling cauldron cooled and deposited its contents into a lidded container complete with easy-pour spout. "It's still coming down in sheets out there. Are you sure you want to look like a drowned cat for the rest of the day?"

"For Hecate's sake, Clarie, haven't you ever heard of an umbrella? And we'll take the path through the woods where it's less wet. Besides, my knees tell me it's about to stop raining."

Unwilling to nix Mag's plans when she was in a rare jovial mood, Clara acquiesced while contemplating how much easier it had been raising a willful daughter with a penchant for trouble than it was dealing with her fully grown, cantankerous sister. Not that she'd trade the opportunity to spend more time with Mag for anything in the world. They'd had enough time apart while Clara passed twenty-five years encased in stone for a crime she didn't commit—and many more years besides, during the decades Mag traveled the world making her name as a rogue Raythe hunter.

Considering how close she'd come to losing her sister altogether, Clara chose to approach Mag with as much patience and understanding as humanly possible. So far, it had netted her a few more gray hairs than she'd have liked, but they'd settled into a companionable—if not always agreeable—relationship and Clara couldn't imagine living without her.

"Your walks tend to take far longer than planned. Get Jinx and Pye to agree to man the shop, and I'll come along." Clara said, giving in.

Halfway down the stairs, the pitter-patter of little paws turned to human footsteps as both familiars answered the call. Pyewacket's human form was as sleek and powerful as her feline one. Tawny skin that shone like velvet deepened across her face to create a natural smoky eyeshadow effect, and when she turned those crystal blues on a male customer, he was sunk. Women responded to her friendly smile and willingness to find the beauty in everyone, and it was a good thing, too.

Since the two Balefire sisters had moved to Harmony, Clara had put most of her magical efforts into creating a personal care product line; a prospect Pye found slightly boring.

Jinx, on the other hand, preferred boring. Left to his own devices, his white, fluffy feline form followed a slow arc across the floor as he followed the hottest sun-warmed spot he could find throughout the day. People interested him less than flies, but Mag paid for his services in the one currency he could not resist. Succulent, juicy tuna.

After finishing lunch, they set out into the gloomy weather. By the time the sage plot came into view, Mag's knees had proved themselves better forecasters than the channel five weatherman, and the umbrella was no longer necessary.

"What in tarnation is going on here?" Mag exclaimed as she took in the decimated crop. "It's all been chewed off at the stem!" She held up a handful of pockmarked leaves for Clara's examination. Mag was right; the entire crop appeared to have been eaten by some kind of bug.

"Caterpillars? Or maybe slugs?" Clara wondered aloud, while a niggling feeling crept into the recesses of her mind. Before she could put the pieces together, a loud buzzing sound claimed the air, and a charm of hummingbirds swooped out of the forest.

"Freeze," Mag hissed, having gone stock-still herself, "those aren't hummingbirds. They're honey pixies, and they can be dangerous in groups, especially during mating season."

Clara did as instructed; she'd learned long ago that when Mag used her big sister voice, it was best to listen. Once, when she was five and approaching an ornery but beautiful phoenix at a fellow witch's birthday party, Clara had ignored a warning just like this one—and wound up with a pair of singed eyebrows, a sizable peck mark on her peaches-and-cream cheek, and a violent dislike for anything with feathers.

Even so, Clara couldn't deny her curiosity and slowly raised her eyes to peer at the tiny creatures. To her surprise, they didn't look at all threatening. In fact, they reminded her of faeries in their miniature form, tiny little bodies with wings that beat so fast she couldn't tell what color they were. One female with cropped hair the color of glittering aquamarine swooped over to Mag, took a sniff, and let out a series of chirps that set the whole flight chattering as they zoomed into the forest and out of sight.

"I guess they didn't think we were a threat. Come on, now." Mag headed toward the path and beckoned Clara to follow.

"Where are we going?"

An exasperated Mag directed an eye roll at her sister, "To find where those pixies went, duh. They aren't here by accident, I can assure you. Native to the Faelands, which means someone—and I have a sneaking suspicion I know exactly who—brought them to our realm."

"Hagatha." Clara and Mag spoke in unison.

"What do you suppose she's got planned?" Clara wondered aloud.

"How in the world should I know? Everything that woman does is a mystery to me. She's not the first thousand-year-old-plus witch I've met, but she's most definitely the nuttiest. No wonder the coven didn't want to deal with her shenanigans anymore."

Clara snorted. "When they called us here to keep tabs on her, I thought it was because they respected the legendary Balefire sisters. After all, I *was* Keeper of the Flame for over a century, and your reputation as a warrior precedes you across realms. But now it just feels like glorified babysitting, and I can't help but wonder if there's a conspiracy behind it all."

The stroke to Mag's ego lightened her feet and the gentle shushing sounds they made in the knee-high grass fed something primitive in her soul. If she wanted to, Mag could lay a hand on the soil and ask Mother Earth to give up her secrets. The connection to the elements came down from mother to daughter or, more rarely, from father to son. Earth, fire, air, and water carried the magic to feed her own and today, the air spoke to her of strange charms and enchantments.

"All the more reason to prove those lazy witches wrong. Listen, I hear something up ahead," Mag said, motioning for Clara to follow her. The brisk pace she set spoke volumes about her level of concern. "I'm going to pay for this later—I hope that batch of hip ointment is almost ready.”

“I’ve got you covered, Maggie. Look, there she is.”

Mag descended upon the old woman who had just wrangled the swarm of honey pixies into a mesh enclosure. Hagatha’s tennis-ball-footed walker stood in the center of a mossy clearing, the sun glinting off its chrome frame. How she’d gotten all the way up the hill with the thing, Clara couldn’t imagine.

“What in Hades are you thinking?” Mag demanded as Hagatha’s eyes bounced between the sisters with no trace of remorse. Looking at the bones of her—which was easy since there wasn’t enough flesh on them to see much of anything else—and squinting a little, it was plain to see that Hagatha had once been a robust and lovely woman. These days, the ones she must be counting as some of her last, the old witch could have been the poster girl for, well, old witches. Wrinkled and wizened, she reminded Clara of a bitten apple left in the sun to dry.

Hagatha could barely contain her excitement despite having gone to great lengths to keep the pixies a secret. “Aren’t they beautiful? Picked up a half dozen from a black-market dealer in the Fringe. Cost me a pretty penny, but I was able to cut the price by half—did you know there are people out there who will pay top dollar for the toenail clippings of a millennial witch?”

“Sure, they’re cute and all,” Mag grudgingly agreed, ignoring the mental image of Hagatha’s bunion-covered toes, “but they breed about ten times faster than bunnies, and they'll need something to feed on. I'd rather it not be all the sage in New England."

"Pish posh!" Hagatha brushed off Mag's warning. "They're going to eat what I brought them here to eat—the black flies, mosquitoes, and midges that have gotten out of control. You should see my backside after every ritual—chewed to shreds, and even if it wasn't cruel, I don't care for the scent of those bug sprays."

She held the mesh enclosure up, smiling at pixies within. "Tea tree oil doesn't seem to deter them any either, and once we start dancing around the fire, all that stuff slides down into my nether regions and stings."

The image of Hagatha dancing skyclad around the ritual fire roared into life behind Clara's eyes, and she wished she had a gallon of brain bleach handy. Mag's pained expression indicated she was thinking the same thing.

"So it's cruel to kill them with bug spray, but it's fine to let a swarm of pixies eat them?" Mag demanded.

Hagatha shrugged. "Circle of life. It's either that or Penelope Starr gets her way, and we nix the naked-dancing custom altogether. Then what's next? Do you have any idea how much tradition we've already lost over the years? It's despicable."

She waved her hand. "Fine, nobody has the stomach to sacrifice a goat anymore; I can live with that. Too squeamish to prick their fingers for a little harmless blood magic; okay, there are a lot more communicable diseases in this day and age, so I'll let it slide. But if this coven takes much more of the magic out of being a witch, we might as well chuck our wands and smother the Balefire. I. Won't. Have. It." She rattled her walker, emphasizing each word.

"You've stirred the entire garden club into a tizzy," Clara said. "A member has already been attacked by one of your little pets, and Angela Sinclair told me they're considering contacting the ornithological association and inviting an expert to weigh in on the problem."

The senior witch merely shrugged and returned to tending the pixies, and Clara sighed, knowing the trouble had only begun.

Chapter Three

"Put that thing away." Clara took her hand off the wheel long enough to shove at the map fluttering into her line of sight. "I'm using the maps app on my phone, and where did you even find a paper version? No one uses them anymore."

A faded teal blue, the VW bus Mag had acquired when they'd moved from the bustling city of Port Harbor hadn't had a working engine, but the Balefire sisters had seen to that with a few waves of their wands. Still, it sputtered with every tap of the gas pedal, and a faded, '70s-era mural gave gawkers the impression that the two elder witches had stolen the original Mystery Machine from Scooby Doo himself.

"If you get to the main entrance to the golf course, you've gone too far." Side-seat driving was Mag's way of punishing Clara for being the one behind the wheel. "Ridge Road runs parallel to the country club."

"I know. I looked it up before we left the house and the customer gave us directions once you settled on a delivery fee." One Clara thought on the high side, but her sister was all about the Benjamins.

"Take the next right. On Ridge Road," Mag announced at the same time as Clara's app suggested the turn. She rustled the map again, squinted at the fine print, and angled it toward a patch of sunlight streaming across the dashboard.

When the colorful sheet blocked Clara's view of the road again, she simply conjured a spark of the magic Balefire from which she took her name and, knowing the heat wouldn't touch her sister's flesh, pointed to the map. It went up like a torch and burned to cinders in under a second.

"I'm trying to drive with some semblance of safety." Clara spun the wheel and rocketed up the road that ran along the southern border of the country club and golf course. The squeak of rubber on heated pavement belied her claim and netted an icy look from Mag, who was holding two shreds of colored paper and a furious expression.

The masculine snort issuing from the cargo space in the rear of the VW bus came from Jinx, who would be providing the muscle during the delivery of an oak dresser aged to a fine, caramel sheen.

Whatever hot retort Mag might have made died on her lips when she spied the red-and-blue eagle emblazoned across the side of the mail truck nestled into a turn-off on her right.

Mag swiveled in her seat and leaned halfway out the window to stare at the blue-uniformed figure of Taylor Dean in the middle of yet another confrontation with a man.

Arms waving, his face a mask of fury, the mailman consumed Mag's attention, so she barely noticed the red truck standing half in the ditch on the other side of the VW as Clara eased on past.

It looked like Taylor had been interrupted in the act of rooting around in the packages stacked up in the open rear hatch. More boxes lay on the ground near the bumper.

"Honestly, the Pony Express did a better job getting the mail delivered on time." Mag should know since she'd lived through part of the evolution leading up to the current postal system. "And don't get me started on that schoolboy uniform."

Shutting Mag off mid-rant was like trying to stuff a cork back in a bottle of champagne while it was still fizzing. You could do it, but it would be messy and not quite worth the effort, so Clara tuned her sister out and tried to enjoy the drive.

Two minutes later, Clara let out a sharp sound and hit the brakes hard enough to send Mag pitching forward.

"Sorry, the road turned to gravel without any warning. You okay back there?" She called out to Jinx. His answering grunt earned a glance in the rearview mirror. Like many cats, Jinx considered a ride in a car as an exercise in torture, only relieved by the occasional bird or squirrel or rabbit sighting.

A washboard texture and potholes big enough to swallow a Buick sucked all Clara's pleasure out of the drive. Banking out of the third in a series of tight turns, she jammed both feet on the brakes again when a figure in a reflective vest waved a stop sign at her.

"At least the road crew is here doing something about the problem," Clara injected false cheer into the comment while Mag continued to sulk over the loss of her map and two jolts against the seat belt. Jinx stared intently out the window. Amid a great deal of beeping and scraping, the grading machine worked on.

And on.

And on.

After ten minutes, Clara started tapping her fingers on the steering wheel, and Mag's desire to complain outran her ability to maintain the silent treatment.

"I'm this close to doing something witchy," she held her thumb and forefinger practically touching. "Come on, we've got places to go, furniture to deliver." The energy level in the bus ticked up a couple of notches to prove she was hitting her limit. "All he has to do is pull over to the side for a minute, and we can go right by. Come on, what's the holdup?" Reaching over, Mag blasted the horn. Or she would have if the horn on the bus had actually been up to the task. The best it could do was a half-hearted, double meep that wouldn't scare a fly.

"Someone else is coming up behind us." Clara caught the movement out her side mirror. "Maybe with two vehicles waiting, they'll be more motivated to let us through."

But it was not to be, Clara realized as the truck eased into the other lane and the driver jumped out. Square was the best word to describe the man. His blocky head sat on wide shoulders without benefit of a neck to break up the shapes.

The temperature went up another degree in the bus, no doubt due to Mag's rising level of annoyance, while the newcomer strutted over to have a word with the sign-waving flag person who, Clara thought, looked about ready to melt under his heavy vinyl vest.

"Hey, isn't that the same guy the mailman was arguing with back there?" Clara said. "It's the same truck I saw parked on the side of the road."

A sign reading Blackthorne Excavation scrolled across the door of a truck that should have been called the *Compensating for Something* model: dual rear wheels, four doors, a huge roll bar covered with lights, all in look-at-me red.

"I guess so. I wasn't paying much attention." Mag admitting she'd missed something happened about as often as a solar eclipse, but Clara decided it was better not to gloat.

No-neck moved on from the flagman to carry on an animated conversation with the driver of the beeping monstrosity that included several gestures toward Mag and Clara. Finally, with a nod, he swaggered over to the side if the VW to have a word.

"Morning ladies." Apparently, Jinx's human form counted for female, but it was Clara who got the cheeky grin and the inevitable downward sliding eye. "I'm Reggie Blackthorne of Blackthorne Excavation. Sorry 'bout the delay. Road needed to be scraped down to the substrate after all that rain. I'll get Charlie to move over so you can go by. Be careful now—it's a little rough going."

Thanking him, Clara drove on. Once they were past any possible chance of being overheard, Mag asked, "Don't you get tired of men talking to your boobs?"

Shrugging, Clara replied, "I entertain myself by imagining what might happen if I enchanted them to respond. I can assure you it's a temptation I work hard to resist."

Destination on the left in 500 feet, the GPS app intoned.

Forty-five minutes later, after the dresser had been moved three times to get it in just the right spot—no, it's no trouble at all, ma'am—Mag left Clara to collect payment and dashed for the driver's seat. She planted her butt there and refused to move, leaving Clara with no choice but to ride shotgun.

The men had made a few hundred more feet of progress with the road scraper before abandoning it on the side of the road, leaving just enough room to slide past. Which Mag did at about twice the speed she should have been going.

"Lunch break." Clara commented after glancing at the position of the sun—no self-respecting Balefire woman ever wore a watch.

"Speaking of," Mag said, grinning. "I could do with a bite. Want to blow the delivery money on seafood?" Her mood much improved by the sale and the thrill of speeding down a back road, Mag was happy for the first time since leaving the shop.

Stretched out in cat form to enjoy the heat from a swath of sun across the back seat, Jinx meowed his agreement, and Clara was outnumbered.

Mag's good mood lasted all of a minute and a half—right up until she spied the familiar square body of the mail truck still sitting in the turnoff. The air literally turned blue and smelled slightly of burnt toast when she loosed a string of curse words.

"It's been over an hour, and he's still screwing around out here?" She spun the wheel, pulled to the side of the road, and jumped out of the driver's seat faster than a woman who looked her age ought to be able to move. Assuming a little diplomacy was about be in order, Clara applied feet to the ground and hurried to intervene.

Rounding the rear corner of the truck, she quickly learned it was already too late. Mag stood over Taylor Dean's body, which was sprawled across the grassy verge.

Clara's breath left her in a whoosh. "Is he dead?"

Sightless eyes stared up at Mag, and she didn't need to go through the formality of testing for a pulse, but she did it anyway. The look on her face told the tale.

"What did you do?"

"Oh, for Hecate's sake, Clara. I didn't kill the poor lout, though I find it illuminating to see what you really think of me." A hundred gallons of water would have evaporated in a flash under the dryness of Mag's tone. "Can't say I wasn't tempted, but you can tell he's been here a while. Hit in the head, I'd say. Maybe with a baseball bat. Something like that." While Clara composed herself, Mag bent to take a closer look. "I guess this means our fruit-of-the-month order is going to be late."

Clara rolled her eyes. "Really, Mag. A little sympathy, please."

"I do feel sorry for him in case you're wondering," Mag said, lifting a shoulder. "Lousy at his job, but no one deserves to go out with the side of his head bashed in like that."

Out of the corner of her eye, Mag caught a flash of white as Jinx's agile body bolted back toward the bus. He must have seen a squirrel or a bird and been unable to resist the thrill of the catch.

"Don't you make a mess on the seats!" She yelled toward the open window and received a plaintive howl in response. The thumping sounds of a cat at play followed, but she turned back toward the business at hand.

Clara was already on the phone. "Ridge Road. Yes, we'll stay right here." She tapped the screen to end the call. "The police are on the way. We're to stay here and guard the scene. And don't touch anything."

That last came a beat too late. Mag had already begun poking around the truck, her sharp gaze taking in details like a hawk. The boxes she'd observed earlier were still piled on the ground behind the open rear door.

One lay on the carpeted floor, flaps open, the contents looking like they'd been rifled through.

Somebody had tossed a roll of packing tape next to it, and there was a second box that had been carefully resealed. If she hadn't seen the man himself in the act of sorting through boxes, this might look like murder followed by theft. Or vice versa.

A shallow, pebble-lined ditch gave way to a low rise bordered by a gravel access track used, Mag could only assume, by the grounds-keeping staff. Beyond that, a sparse band of trees divided the road from the country club proper. A pair of muddy gouges about the width of a golf cart trailed between a pair of young maples to intersect with the access track.

"Look here." Mag navigated the shallow incline and pointed to clumps of mud spit out by tire treads onto the drier surface below. "I'd bet you anything the killer left those wheel marks. Get out that infernal device of yours and get some pictures. You never know, we might need them. The tracks, the body, the truck. I want it all."

"The police are on their way," the distant wail of sirens proved it true, "why don't we leave this to them?"

"I have a feeling, Clarie. One of my flutters. The ones I used to get when it was time to go on the hunt. I'm needed." She paused. "We're needed, I suppose." The excitement brought back the glitter Clara remembered from her youth. Margaret Balefire had always had the shine. More than any other witch she'd ever known, and there was no way her sister would stand in the way if Mag felt a compulsion to act.

"Okay, I'll do it." Maybe Mag's excitement was contagious, but Clara could feel a few flutters of her own. Snapping shot after shot, she recorded the entire scene and slid the phone into her pocket as the first black-and-white skidded into view.

Chief Cobb's eyebrows shot to his hairline then dropped into a scowl when he saw who was waiting for him at the scene of the murder.

"Well, you ladies certainly do seem to find trouble everywhere you go. Might make a thinking man wonder what it is you been up to."

Mag's quiet snort revealed her opinion of him as a thinking man and Clara treated her sister to a quelling look.

"What were you doing way out here anyway?" Cobb squatted down to check the mailman's pulse even though it was clear there would be nothing to find. Clara caught the brief expression of compassion flitting across his face, and it made her think a little bit better of him.

"We were out here to deliver a dresser to the house at the end of the road," Clara replied. "Mr. Dean was alive and well about an hour ago when we passed by. It looked like he'd been rearranging the packages in the rear of the truck."

"And he was alone? Did you see anyone else on the road?" Holding up a finger to keep the sisters from answering, Cobb listened to dispatch giving him an ETA on impending backup, then continued, "I want you to think carefully and tell me everything you saw."

"As a matter of fact," Clara said, "he was arguing with Reggie Blackthorne when we passed. It couldn't have been much of a fight, though, because a few minutes later, Mr. Blackthorne pulled up behind us and had a word with the road crew.”

Mag added, “Then he came over to introduce himself to us, explained why the crew was taking so long, and they finally let us through after making us sit there for at least ten minutes.”

“Do you remember how many men or women were part of the road crew?” Cobb raised an eyebrow at Mag’s tart tone but kept his even and professional.

“Four, I think,” Mag said, holding his gaze, “but they left during the time we spent delivering the desk.”

“Which took?”

“Forty-five minutes give or take,” Clara said.

“Plus another fifteen waiting for the workers to clear the road,” Mag fumed inwardly just thinking about it but kept a level tone.

Backup arrived with more lights and sirens and a rush of activity.

“Stay here. I’ll send someone to take an official statement. You didn’t touch anything did you?”

“Checked for a pulse and then called you straightaway,” Mag lied without batting so much as an eyelash.

Cobb assigned a young officer by the name of Lynn Nye to interview Mag and Clara. Bright-eyed and eager, Nye looked like she had just exited the Academy and this might be her first assignment. Every few seconds, her eyes slid toward where the body lay, and she swallowed hard, but to her credit, the young woman conducted a thorough questioning.

Over the next half hour, she took both women through the series of events at least three times. While mechanically answering question after question, Mag tuned her attention to the crew's chatter.

"Blunt force trauma delivered with a long-handled weapon. Golf club, if I had to make an immediate guess. Makes sense, given the location." The coroner reported to Chief Cobb, who answered with a short nod and a sidelong glance in Mag and Clara's direction.

After what felt like an age, Mag's stomach rumbled so hard it hurt, and she was tired of watching while the police cordoned off the scene and rushed about collecting evidence.

"We've told you everything we know. You have our contact information. If there's nothing else, we'll be leaving now." Leaning heavily on her cane, Mag dared the officer to detain her further, and yelled back over one shoulder, "You coming, Clara?"

Seeing no other choice, Officer Nye dismissed the Balefires with a warning not to leave town.

Chapter Four

A few days after the murder, the shop was hopping, and all anyone could talk about was the death of the mailman. Except for one lady, a statuesque woman with piercing blue eyes and a full mane of graying hair who couldn't be bothered to bring up the subject. Full of single-minded purpose, she scanned the room until her gaze fell on an artful display of items featuring dried lavender.

"Is that culinary or ornamental?" She waved a slim-fingered but capable hand at a bowl of the fragrant potpourri Clara sold by the ounce. "I'm looking for English lavender, the Munstead variety," she said. "Food grade, please. Clean and dry, with no added oils to increase or prolong the scent. For cooking."

Smiling, Clara asked, "Would you prefer fresh-picked or dried? All our ingredients are organic, most grown right here in our own backyard. We cultivate a wide variety of herbs for use in our products. I'd be happy to take you on a tour of the greenhouse and gardens. I'm Clara Balefire, by the way."

At ease now, the woman relaxed and introduced herself. "Nice to meet you. Name's Maude, and I'm an avid baker, and I'd love to see what you have back there. I'm making a pear galette, and I thought it might be nice to infuse the dough with fragrant lavender." She sighed. "Unfortunately, I've lost my entire crop this year to the damnable hummingbirds. I'll just take some of the dried today, but I'll come back sometime for a few sprigs of fresh if you don't mind selling them that way."

"Anytime. If you'll wait just one moment, I have a lovely batch in the back." Clara passed through the storeroom to the garden behind and selected a scant handful of fresh, fragrant spears. Calling a wisp of Balefire into her palm, she directed the heat toward the tender leaves and petals, drying them so gently they lost none of their scent.

A whiff of magic stripped away everything but the pale-colored flowers, and these she whisked into a paper cone already stamped with the store logo, twisted the top, and tied it with a ribbon.

Maude accepted the parcel, lifted it to her nose to sniff with appreciation, then paid with a smile.

"Now, if you'd like to follow me we can take that tour of the greenhouse. I really think you'll—"

An excited murmur arose between three perfectly-coiffed ladies in the process of haggling over who would get to buy one of Mag's Hummel figurines. Each woman was convinced she'd seen it first, and a lively discussion ensued. They were no closer to a decision, though quite near to wearing on Mag's last nerve.

"That's Babette Dean, and it looks like she's headed this way," a lady with owl-eye glasses said in a stage whisper, her gaze drawn to a woman outside on the strip of walkway visible through the shop window.

"Didn't expect to see her out and about so soon. Not after the way her husband was killed. I heard they had to use dental records to identify the body because there was so much damage to his face."

Mag took a breath to refute that salacious bit of gossip, then thought better of it. Why answer questions when all she had to do was stay quiet and let them believe a load of baloney?

"I heard the cops are looking at her for the murder."

"Well, I heard he was mobbed up. Come on." The ringleader—the one Mag had nicknamed Ms. Fancy Pants because of the sheer weight she carried in gold jewelry—dragged the other two ladies into a secluded spot where they could listen without being spotted.

"If you'll excuse me," Maude said, looking out the window, "I've decided against a tour of the greenhouse today. I'll come back another time if you don't mind. I'm terribly interested to learn what other culinary delights might be growing out there, but I just remembered an appointment, and I must go." She sailed out the door.

If Clara found anything odd about Maude's behavior, it went right out of her head because she was more interested in meeting Babette Dean and hearing her story than taking someone around the gardens.

The bell over the door tinkled, and a hush fell over the three women crammed in a corner when the newly widowed Babette entered the store. She was a narrow woman, was all Clara could think, but not in a wiry or willowy way, just narrow as if a line ran down her center and every part of her angled back from there. Only her eyes were wide, their deep blue framed with the redness left by an ocean of tears in an otherwise pale face.

Not as wide, though, as Mag's eyes went when her gaze fell on the box dangling from Babette's right hand. Mahogany with a decorative rosewood inlay and brass bindings, it looked too old and too valuable to be carried in such a careless manner. Giving it a mighty heave, the tiny woman raised Mag's heart rate another notch when she dropped the box on the counter with a bang.

"You sell antiques, so I was wondering if—I mean would you have any interest in maybe purchasing this box? I don't know much about it, except it's old and my"—her voice went hoarse—"husband told me it was worth a lot of money. He's gone and I … it was unexpected. There are going to be costs and the insurance will take time."

"That's a writing box, circa 1870." Mag's tone drew Clara's attention. Something was wrong, and Babette was at the heart of it, but for once, it seemed Mag chose diplomacy in place of a hissy fit. Stepping closer, Clara caught Mag's eye and received a dark look in exchange.

"It's worth about twelve hundred dollars. I could give you a thousand because I need to make at least some profit on it." Calm and cool on the outside, Mag seethed under the surface. Clara sensed it but didn't understand the reason.

"Yes. Yes, that would be fine. I didn't expect it to be that much. Thank you. I'm just … thank you." Tears welled fresh. Babette cleared her throat, sniffled a couple of times, then pulled herself back together while a suspiciously silent Mag wrote out a purchase order and pulled cash from the till.

Unable to see such misery without trying to do something to help, Clara made her way over to the pie safe that doubled as a display case. A moment passed while she considered the best choice, then she pulled a box of her famous tension-reducing herbal tea blend from the shelf. She let a tendril of magic slide out to taste Babette's energy. The tea would take some of the edge off, but not even the most magically gifted witch could alter the depth and breadth of grief.

"Take this. It's an herbal blend. Steep it for ten minutes and drink a cup whenever you start to feel overwhelmed. I truly am sorry for your loss." Babette's fingers felt chilled despite the heat of the day. No wonder she wore a long-sleeved top in the middle of summer.

Babette accepted the tea and fumbled in her purse for cash.

"On the house," Clara waved away the payment.

Instead of turning to leave, Babette paused as though there were something more she wanted to say.

"Is there something else I can do for you, dear?" Clara asked while Mag stashed the rosewood box underneath the counter. Whatever it was that had her sister seething, Babette seemed lost, and Clara's heart went out to her.

"No. Not really. It's just that you're so nice to me and people have been saying such horrible things about my Taylor. And about me, and I'm rattling around in the house alone. My mother came for a few days, but she's gone now, and I don't know what to do with myself. Your shop is so warm and welcoming. Would it be okay if I browse a little?"

The furtive shuffling of feet sounded from the corner where the three women were hiding. They probably hadn't expected Babette to hang around, and they were trying to figure out whether to come out or stay hidden. Clara felt no sympathy for them. Being on the wrong end of unearned speculation was something she and Babette had in common.

Combining Margaret's love of antiques with Clara's affinity for creating lotions and creams turned the interior of Balms and Bygones into an eclectic haven of sights and smells. Under the earthy notes of Clara's signature lines lay hints of beeswax, lemon, and antique wood. Jewel-toned jars sparkled on the patina of old things Mag kept polished to a shine.

No one who knew them, least of all the Balefire sisters themselves, would have placed bets on this shop becoming a labor of love, or on Mag managing to serve the public without adding a new toad or two to the world. But so far, so good.

Until today with Babette, who seemed prone to touching. She ran a finger over a crystal decanter, and Mag simmered like she carried an active volcano inside and was about to blow. After two suppressed sighs and a full-on snort, Clara sent her sister a questioning look.

"Get her out of here," Mag mouthed back, but it was too late. In a feat it would have taken a group of engineers with precision timing to carry off, Babette tested the texture of a fist-sized cannonball. The gentle touch sent it rolling off the shelf and onto the up-ended tines of a fork lying in a shallow tray. The fork flipped up, levered a spoon and sent it flying with sufficient force to knock into the curved handle of an umbrella in its stand. The handle spun in an arc that swept it across the edge of a dresser and caught on one of Mag's famous tatted doilies.

Mag saw it coming, but while she possessed the magic to reverse the whole debacle, there stood Babette, right in the middle of the fray, leaving her no choice but to let it all play out. Still, she averted her gaze when a prized crystal vase teetered on the brink of destruction.

Clara lunged, measuring her length upon the floor, and caught the vase a breath away from the hardwood surface. The sound of her elbows cracking against the hard oak flooring made Babette wince with pain.

"Oh, I'm so sorry. I'm such a klutz." When Babette reached down to help, her sleeves slid up to reveal a series of bruises on one arm that were just fading from purple into yellow around the edges. "I'm always knocking things over and bumping into things—doors, furniture." She yanked the cloth back down to cover the vicious-looking marks and made a hasty retreat.

No sooner had the door closed behind her when, chattering like magpies, the three women vacated their hidden corner.

"I thought she'd never leave. I can't believe you talked me into hiding back there for so long." The ringleader ignored the fact it had been her idea in the first place.

"To be honest, I'm starting to feel a little sorry for talking about her that way. She seemed so lost and alone." Owl-glasses earned herself a discount on the Hummel for that.

Looking like she was about to burst, Mag rang up the purchase, pulled two more of a similar vintage out of storage, and sent the gossip brigade out the door. The second it swung shut behind them, she rounded on Clara

"Babette Dean just sold me my own writing box. The one I bought from that widow down in Charleston, remember? I packed it up myself and had it shipped here, but it never came."

"Are you sure? There must be hundreds of them out there, just like that one."

"You are aware there weren't writing box factories in the late 1800s, right? These were not mass-produced. And yes, I'm sure it's the same box. I'd know it anywhere."

Mag spread a towel on the counter, retrieved the writing box, and laid it gently down on the lid.

"See this rub mark? And that crack that runs along the joint? I documented both on the receipt. Looks like the mailman has been stealing packages, and that's a federal offense. Makes sense now why he was out on that back road digging around in boxes. What a jerk."

"Well, I don't suppose he can be convicted of it now, considering he's dead. You don't think Babette knew anything about it, do you?" Clara sincerely hoped not, but you never knew.

"I can't see how she would be stupid enough to bring that particular piece to me if she had any idea that it was stolen property. I wish I had asked her if she had any more things she wanted to sell. If he's done this more than once and someone found out, it could speak to motive."

That was Mag, always thinking about bringing the bad guy to justice, and it was certainly more plausible than the theory that he was mobbed up.

"Love, money, or revenge. Those are the three most common motives for murder, and did you notice no one said anything about him stepping out on his wife? That leaves money and revenge."

While she talked, Mag kept her hands busy polishing the brass with a microfiber cloth. "But we can't discount the bat-crap-crazy factor."

"So you think there's a sociopath loose in the town of Harmony? Unlikely." Or maybe Clara just wanted to believe the best of people.

Mag lifted a shoulder. "Stranger things have happened." Given her history, the term *stranger things* took on a whole other level of meaning.

"If the cops really are looking at Babette, we shouldn't rule out love as a motive just yet. Maybe she caught him catting around with a neighbor or something. Those bruises on her arms didn't look self-inflicted. Maybe he was an abusive husband."

"Then it would be a case of self-defense. Who could blame her?"

Clara tossed out two or three more theories before she noticed Mag wasn't paying any attention to the conversation. She'd flipped the inlaid box back over and opened the lid to reveal a series of compartments and a sloped writing space. Running reverent fingers over the polished wood, Mag tested the dividers to make sure none were loose. She ignored her sister until Clara finally trailed off on her lit list of possible reasons for killing the mailman.

"I wonder if this one has a secret ..." A secret what, Clara would not learn right then because the leader of the Hummel brigade had returned on her own to ask if Mag had any other treasures stashed away.

Chapter Five

"It's not normal," and it wasn't the first time Mag had stated this particular opinion, either. "A coven that meets in the middle of town. Where's the nature? The elements?" Even the tapping of her cane on the sidewalk sounded annoyed.

For thousands of years, witches have practiced their craft in secret, meeting on the sly to conceal magic from the rest of the world. While that may seem unfair to those not blessed with mystical power, so does the persecution witches have suffered at the hands of regular humans throughout the ages.

Hagatha Crow had already lived through several such periods, and the effects of the Salem witch trials had still been fresh when she enlisted the Harmony coven to form a civic organization aptly named The Moonstone Circle. Hiding in plain sight, the coven operated behind the scenes while contributing to the community in a myriad of ways.

Of course, then-Pastor Evaniah Johnson had to stick his nose in and create the Brotherhood of Badgers, relegating the Moonstones to the status of an auxiliary group. Hagatha considered the act a blatant attempt to further usurp the good women of Harmony's independence and retaliated with a curse that affected old Evaniah's tender regions and encouraged a rivalry between the two groups that had yet to be laid to rest.

If it had been up to Haggie, the Moonstones would have continued on their way, happily spitting in the Badgers' faces while performing their rites and rituals as tradition dictated. Instead, she'd passed the civic baton to Penelope Starr, who had allowed the title of First Chair to go straight to her head, and assumed that meant she also held dominion over the coven itself—whether she was next in line for the job or not.

By rights, the designation of High Priestess should have passed on to Gertrude Granger who, at half Hagatha's age, was still the next-oldest coven member. However, she lived all year with the spirit of Christmas in her heart and was too focused on whether or not the great wizard known as Santa Claus had noticed her efforts to spread holiday cheer. Instead, she spent most of her time giving back to the less fortunate through one of her many charitable causes.

"Hello, you two," She mumbled around the candy cane stuck between her teeth. To describe Gertrude, one need only evoke the curious image of a pin-up girl slightly past her prime and dressed as a Christmas elf. That night, green velvet stretched over her prodigious bosom and barely skimmed over her behind. White tights spangled with glitter completed the look.

Since arriving in Harmony, Gertrude had been one of the only coven members to accept the Balefire sisters with open arms. Even though Mag thought her a bit eccentric, Clara was happy to see that she'd had arrived at the coven meeting early and saved them two seats in a prime location near the air conditioning vent.

Convening indoors smacked of blasphemy to Mag, who felt the municipal building's conference room lacked ambiance. Clara had quelled her complains with a diatribe, insisting the location was acceptable only because that day's meeting would focus more on planning and less on ritual.

Gertrude's eyes were kindly, and her painted and glossed lips curved into a soft smile as Clara and Mag took their seats.

The rap of Penelope's gavel might as well have been nails on a chalkboard as far as Mag was concerned. It was enough to make her miss the mysteriously absent Hagatha. Penelope was smart enough to know that their high priestess never arrived at coven meetings on time, but had insisted the topic at hand was so urgent it couldn't possibly wait for their leader's arrival.

"Silence, please." She urged when the majority of the rest of the group—sixteen witches in total—continued their cheery chitchat. Only the two women flanking Penelope—her henchwomen, Mabel Youngblood and Evanora Dupree—refrained from speaking.

Mouths set in thin, disapproving lines, the three of them looked like they were auditioning for the adult version of Mean Girls. How a trio of women who had lived through the civil war and the industrial revolution could maintain any level of self-respect while acting like adolescents was beyond Mag's comprehension.

Penelope, who had mastered the art of glamour to present her best face to the non-magically inclined, had not been blessed with either beauty or brains. The fact that she kept up the facade in a room full of witches who could always see the sour expression hiding underneath spoke volumes about her ego.

Furthermore, it didn't appear that her centuries on earth had granted her the admirable quality of maturity, which—it could be argued—might have rendered a variety of her other personality traits bearable. Still, she was one of the most gifted conjurers Mag had ever seen, though it felt like chewing chalk to admit it.

"First on the docket," Penelope began.

"What are we, in court?" Mag muttered under her breath, earning a giggle from Clara and three sharp glares from the front of the room.

Penelope continued as if she hadn't been interrupted. "Is the matter of Bobbie-Sue Abernathy, who wishes to join the Moonstones. I am aware that this is a sensitive topic, but I believe it warrants a discussion. Clearly, there is something special about this woman, considering she has continued to request admission even through our deterrent charms and enchantments."

Mag shot Clara a mischievous grin and raised her voice in rebuttal, "Isn't this supposed to be a coven meeting? Why are we discussing Circle business? You don't honestly expect us to invite a human into the coven, do you?"

Penelope sighed, shook her head, and began speaking as though to a child. "Settle down, please.

Bobbie-Sue comes from an influential family and would, I believe, be an asset to our charity work. Besides which, we've had a request from the leader of our brother organization to apply some leniency."

"Brother organization," Mag muttered. "Whoever heard of such a thing?"

Ignoring Mag, Penelope spoke to the rest of the coven. "Perry said he would consider it a personal favor if we relaxed the rules and let in someone new. He has no reason to suspect there's more behind the Moonstones than meets the eye, and it's becoming ever more difficult to defend our position on increasing membership."

Nothing made Mag's blood come to a boil quite as quickly as being told to calm herself, and though Clara would have preferred to intervene before her sister started throwing the magics around, she knew better than to attempt any sort of countermeasure while the vein in Mag's forehead throbbed like a bongo drum.

"That's the stupidest thing I ever heard. Unless you're considering disbanding the coven to move forward with the secular side of things, the answer is no."

As Mag seethed, Clara looked around the room, noting which witches might enjoy watching Penelope being taken down a peg and which ones would follow her into the ninth level of hell. She judged it at about sixty/forty with a pliable contingency of younger witches on the fence.

"We have no valid reason for refusal, and the last thing I want is to be at odds with Perry Weatherall."

"To Hades with Perry Weatherall! We don't answer to the Brotherhood of Badgers, and even if we did, he could be dispatched easily enough." Clara remained calmly seated while her sister pushed her chair back and raised her fist to the sky, dandelion-fluff hair charged with static electricity and waving about her head. It was a miracle Penelope had gotten off more than two sentences before Mag's frustration bubbled out of her mouth.

"The same way poor Taylor Dean was dispatched?" Penelope shot back with a raised eyebrow.

Clara held her breath, waiting for a deluge that never came. Had Penelope really just insinuated that she or her sister had something to do with the mailman's death?

"I'm going to choose to ignore that last statement considering that if I *were* to murder someone, you can bet your broom nobody would ever know about it. And I certainly wouldn't use a golf club or be found standing over the body. Penelope, with all due respect"—Mag's tone indicated a penny would cover it and still have change coming back—"I believe you're speaking out of turn. You're not our high priestess, and I think we should all wait for Hagatha to arrive before delving into this matter."

Ahh, the high road—and just when Clara had been expecting some entertainment. Titters of agreement echoed throughout the space while Penelope's jaw nearly hit the floor.

"I couldn't agree more." Hagatha's voice rang out above what would have been an audible din if Penelope hadn't already put the kibosh on unsanctioned chatter.

Thump. Tap.

Thump. Tap.

The rhythm of Hagatha's progress pulled the focus of every witch in the room. Clara wondered if, like her sister, who conveniently forgot to use her cane when it behooved her to do so, Hagatha also exaggerated the effects of advancing age. A tiny smile played across her lips as she slowly made her way to the front of the room, noting the expressions of exasperation some of the witches failed to conceal.

"Put that gavel down, Penelope. For Hecate's sake." She silenced the meddling witch whose mouth hung open like a goldfish. It had become such a frequent expression, Mag half considered loosing a curse to render it permanent. Instead, she tamped down the inclination while adding the latest instance of Penelope's insubordination to a running tab that would rival Santa's naughty list.

Gertrude would be so proud.

"First of all," Hagatha continued, "Bobbi-Sue Abernathy can take a flying leap. Strap her to Perry Weatherall's back and kill two birds with one stone. The discussion is closed, permanently.

"Secondly, this coven has always been considered a family, which means we don't accuse one another of heinous acts of evil such as murder. I don't care how new the Balefire sisters are, they're seasoned witches, and

Clara served as High Priestess to one of the Port Harbor groups for years before her unfortunate incarceration."

Gertrude nodded in agreement and stood up to address the group, "We're lucky to have Mag and Clara here. You should be ashamed of yourselves, treating them with that level of contempt. They've done nothing but what they were invited here to do, and you'd all do well to remember that."

"Yes, indeed. They've done a fantastic job corralling your senile leader, haven't they?" Hagatha grinned.

"What?" she asked innocently, enjoying the looks of panic flitting across the faces of Penelope and her flying monkeys. "Didn't think I had any idea about your little coup, did you? I may be old, and I may have lost my give-a-damn for hiding in the shadows, but that doesn't mean I'm off my rocker quite yet. You've got another hundred years of Hagatha ahead of you, at least, I can promise you that.

"Now, if we're all done with the gossip and intrigue, could we couch the civic conversation and actually discuss the upcoming solstice?"

Nobody would have dared argue, even if provided with a leg to stand on, and the meeting moved forward.

"I'm proud of you, Maggie. You really kept your cool in there. What gives? I nearly loosed an acne charm all over Penelope's face, and you were suspiciously magic-less."

Her sister merely shrugged, "All in good time, Clarie." An ominous statement coming from Margaret Balefire.

Clara led Mag out the back door and toward the rear of the municipal building, where a winding path that snaked through the woods would deposit them in their own backyard. As they rounded the corner, Mag noticed a figure moving in their direction.

"Incoming," she hissed under her breath to Clara. "Your biggest fan approaches."

Sure enough, when Clara looked up, it was into the face of Norm McCreery, who Mag referred to as Mayor McCreepy due to his growing obsession with Clara. The fact that he had suspicions of the magical underpinnings of the Moonstone Circle made each of their encounters somewhat awkward, considering the Balefires initially came to town to keep such information under wraps.

Clara thought it might work to their advantage when dealing with human society to have someone on the inside, but wasn't willing to open the door any more than a crack for fear the mayor would try to wedge his way into her life, heart, and bed. None of which she had any interest in, whatsoever.

If you asked, that was her story, and she was sticking to it.

"Mr. Mayor," Clara nodded as he approached.

"Just Norm, please." It wasn't the first time the request had been made.

She dipped her head. "Norm then. What can we do for you?"

"Well, I'm actually trying to do something for you," The mayor turned toward Mag, "I'm sorry to say I was obliged to corroborate Leonard Wayland's statement that you and Taylor Dean had an unpleasant encounter on the sidewalk in front of your place the day before he was murdered."

He cleared his throat. "I want you to know that I don't believe either one of you had anything to do with the crime, but Chief Cobb feels differently. You're not the only suspects he's pursuing if it makes you feel any better."

That piece of news came as no shock to either of the sisters and didn't appear to concern Mag in the least. "You mean Reggie Blackthorne, don't you?"

"No, Reggie has been cleared of all suspicion. There was an altercation, but the facts didn't line up with the time of the murder. That's all the detail I can provide."

He wanted to say more; was practically dying to spill his guts.

"Thanks for the heads up, but since neither of us knew the man well enough to want to kill him, we have nothing to worry about."

"Who are the other suspects?" Clara hoped the desire to impress her would further loosen Mayor McCreery's lips.

"Officially, anyone present at the country club that day, aside from the staff, who have all been cleared." With a pained expression Clara understood to mean he was about to do something he normally wouldn't, Norm continued, "Unofficially, we're looking at the wife. Babette Dean."

"Not very original; it's always the spouse who's fingered." Mag ignored the snort brought on by her unfortunate choice of words. "And what about Leonard himself? He had more words with Taylor than I did. Even you can attest to that."

"And that's exactly what I told the chief. But Leonard was standing in front of a classroom full of high-school geometry students at the time of the murder, so his alibi is iron-clad. Don't worry—they'll find the real culprit eventually. Unless you two find him first." Mayor McCreery left them with that tidbit of information, wondering whether his words were intended as encouragement or merely an observation.

Chapter Six

"What am I supposed to wear to this hen party?" A closet half full of new clothes, and none of them appealed to Margaret Balefire. Where were the bold patterns, the exaggerated paisleys and bright colors of her favorite era? And what was up with the snug legs on those hideous jeans Clara had forced her to buy?

Nothing said fashion like the gentle swish of faded, bell-bottomed denim. She'd worn her hair long back in the day—long enough to brush across the back of her derriere. A mighty fine one she'd had, too. What she wouldn't give for a pair of platform shoes with a chunky heel. Now her closet screamed blah.

"It's not a hen party, it's a social event," Clara said, scowling. "Crocheting for Charity sounded like a fun way to meet more new people. You like to fool with yarn. I'd have thought this would be enjoyable for you."

"Knit. I knit. I don't crochet. You know there's a difference, right?" Defiant, Mag shoved the new clothes aside and grabbed the ugliest thing she could find. A shapeless, flowered polyester number with a zipper down the front that was never meant to be worn in public. The muumuu was the seventies version of today's pajama pants. She ran a hand through wisps of hair to make it stand more on end than normal and marched out of her bedroom.

Clara arched a brow at her. "What? You couldn't find your velour tracksuit?"

"Shut up or I'll carry a polka-dotted parasol and wear my garden boots." Neon pink and covered with butterflies, the boots would set off the ensemble with just the right eccentric touch to make sure Mag was never invited back. Exactly what she wanted, and reason enough to give the addition to her outfit some serious consideration.

"Go ahead," Clara called her bluff. "People will come from miles around to buy antiques from the nutty old bat in Harmony. I'm sure they'll take your prices seriously and not try to haggle you down to the last penny."

"Someone has an acid tongue." Still, Mag was wearing the polyester monstrosity—sans parasol or boots—when Clara led the way into the back room at the Harmony town library. When they came to a thick maple door with a hand-lettered sign reading *Crocheting for Charity* taped to its glass, they knew they were in the right place.

"Looks like a hen party to me," Mag muttered as Clara swung open the door.

Gertrude Granger sat on a folding chair half buried in a candy-cane-patterned scarf that would probably have been too long for the Jolly Green Giant. When she caught sight of the new arrivals, she used widened eyes and a series of subdued head movements to direct their attention to the woman sitting to her right.

Mag chose to ignore Gertrude. She slumped into the first empty space she came to where she could put her back to the wall and have a good view of the entire room. Even here, where the most dangerous thing she might encounter would be a vicious piece of gossip, Mag remained ever vigilant. Thirty seconds later, she defiantly dared anyone to comment on the clack of her knitting needles amid a room full of the shushing sounds made by crochet hooks.

Settling in on Gertrude's left, Clara prepared to introduce herself to the group, but never got the chance.

"You must be Clara Balefire, and that's your mother, right? You'll have to tell me how you managed to get into the Moonstones so quickly. I've been trying for simply ages, and you just show up in town, and you're in. I'd love to know your secret." Young, ruthlessly blond, and perky, but with an avid edge.

Wouldn't you just? Clara considered her initial impression of Bobbie-Sue as Gertrude's questing elbow tagged her on the arm.

"Old family connections." Ancient ones.

"Really? In Harmony? To whom? If you don't mind my asking."

Clara paused to note Bobbie-Sue's body language. A subtle quirk of the brow pursed lips, and a slight upward angle to the chin showed disbelief and gave the impression that she knew, or thought she knew, more than she was willing to say. It left Clara with the unsettled feeling of being put under a microscope, and she pulled out the one name least likely to be questioned.

"Hagatha Crow."

Not only did the name work like magic, it was magic. Hagatha's magic, in fact. It prickled over Clara's skin, leaving a familiar sense of recognition behind. Bobbie-Sue went slack-jawed—only for a second, but when she spoke again, it was on the subject of crocheting.

Gertrude made a quiet sound low in her throat, and Mag's head came up as she scented the magic in the air. It was a powerful spell that could be triggered by the mere mention of a name.

"Tell me about your project," Clara directed her attention toward the crocheter seated directly across from her: Maude Prescott, the woman who had requested dried lavender and a tour of Clara's greenhouse at Balms and Bygones. The crinkly sound of plastic strips twisting and twirling around a massive crochet hook drew curiosity. "What are you making?"

"Sleeping mats for the homeless to help keep them a little warmer at night. It's a double crochet pattern in a simple rectangle shape. Quick and easy to do. We've perfected a method for making them thicker by stacking a pair of mats together and binding them with single crochet around the outside edges. They're lightweight but provide some extra insulation. We box them up by the dozen and drop them off at shelters in Port Harbor once a month."

If she'd had to bet, Clara would put money on Maude having had a brush with homelessness at some point. Steadfast fingers moved through the repetitive motion with a level of conviction. Maybe a family member would benefit from the work.

"We're working to double our quota from last year. Afghans and hats, too."

Mag's knitting needles suddenly got quieter, and Claire noted the chagrined look on her sister's face. Clearly, Mag hadn't expected the group to be doing anything of a seriously charitable nature.

Talk turned to the chatty type that women engage in when there are no men around to listen.

Someone in front of her said, "I hear the club poached that new massage therapist from Back in Touch. He'd only been there a week, and they offered him a double salary to leave without notice."

Fingers flying, Clara listened to the conversation flowing around her without trying to put names to faces.

"Well, can you blame them?" another woman responded. "I mean, the man has the hands of an angel."

"And the backside of a devil." Hoots of laughter followed the ribald comment.

"I've just about had it with the club." Maude Prescott's voice rose to a level of pique that did pull Clara's focus. "I've been a member there for years. Long enough to have a standing tee time and I always use cart number thirty-two. Everyone knows that's my cart. Everyone."

Murmurs of polite, but disinterested sympathy followed, but Maude couldn't let it go. "Then along comes Miriam May in a pair of pants so tight you can see Boston *and* France."

Having lost count of her stitches, Maude paused to yank out an inch of work, then jammed the hook back in place and kept crocheting.

And complaining.

"There used to be a dress code, but that's gone the way of the world. Now, all it takes is a couple of women showing off their wares, waggling their fingers at the attendant, and off they go in my cart. Can you imagine?"

Maude might have continued ranting if a figure hadn't materialized on the other side of the glass.

The door swung open, and a red-eyed Babette Dean entered the room, sniffed once, and bravely said, "Sorry I'm late. I've just returned from talking to the police." Visibly shaken and pale as milk, she focused on one of two empty chairs left in the room and only tripped over one pair of legs before she landed in it.

"Sorry. I'm so sorry." Babette patted her sides as if looking for something, "I didn't even bring my crochet bag. I'm so scattered."

Clara and her sister exchanged a pointed look; it was no surprise to them that Chief Cobb and his new deputy had put the screws to Babette. If the good mayor were correct, they'd soon turn their attention to the Balefires.

Gertrude pierced Babette with a curious stare that Mag guessed, if they hadn't been in public, might have turned into a compulsion spell, eager as she was to find out all the dirty details of the interrogation. "What did the police want? Did they find out who … you know?"

Babette looked at the faces that were turned in her direction, the prying eyes of her unapologetic neighbors, and let loose a wail that could have woken the dead. Mag hadn't thought the woman had it in her, and despite her reservations regarding Babette's innocence, her heart went out to the woman. Not, mind you, that she would have openly admitted the fact.

"They think I hit my own husband over the head with a golf club! Kept asking me where I stashed my set, and wouldn't listen when I told them I don't even play. I was in the steam room, barely a stone's throw from where my husband was being brutally murdered at the time."

Breathing as if she'd been running, Babette seemed determined to get the whole story off her chest.

"Suspicious, they said, that nobody can corroborate my story. How is it my fault the steam room is deserted at that time of day? If only I'd kept my massage appointment, then I'd have an iron-clad alibi, and none of this would be happening." Babette lamented, her voice having reached a pitch that could have cut glass.

"To add insult to injury, they said some horrible things about my Taylor. As if my heart isn't broken already, now every tongue in town is going to be wagging."

"What kinds of things, dear?" Gertrude prodded without remorse. Clara wanted to smack the tinsel right out of her head but dialed it down to a seething glare that did absolutely nothing to stop Gertrude's fishing attempt. After all, what better place to start the tongue-wagging?

"Just…terrible things. That he was a scoundrel, a cheat, a thief. All Taylor ever did was try to give me the life he thought I deserved. And now all he's going to be remembered for are these lies." Tears rolled down Babette's cheeks. "And the worst part of all is Chief Cobb had the nerve to insinuate that my husband beat me, which is ludicrous. Taylor never laid a hand on me. He loved me, and he was the best husband I could have asked for."

Maude cast a sidelong glance at Babette but appeared to follow the adage that if you couldn't say anything nice, you shouldn't say anything at all.

Gertrude apparently had no such filter. "You do tend to look a fright, Babette. We've seen the bruises."

"Gertrude!" Clara's voice rang out with authority. She'd had enough. "Leave the poor woman alone. Can't you see she's distraught?"

Heavily chagrined, Gertrude shut her mouth with a snap. "Of course, I'm sorry. I don't know what got into me. It's all right, Babette. I'm sure they'll find the real killer, and things will be put to rights."

Mag didn't think even finding the killer would redeem Taylor's reputation, but that was a thought better saved for later discussion.

Babette mouthed a silent "thank you" to Clara, and business carried on as usual.

When the crochet hooks had been stowed, and the group had filed out of the library, Babette hung back to have a word with the Balefire sisters.

"Thank you for that. I do want you to know since you've been so nice, that what I said before is the honest-to-God's truth. I happen to be anemic which, among other things, causes my skin to bruise easily. Doesn't help that I'm also clumsy. Taylor used to ask me where each one came from, but I can never remember. I'm always banging into something." She seemed desperate for anyone to believe her, and Clara's heart went out to the woman.

"Babette, I'm sorry to tell you this, but my mother and I were the ones who found Taylor's body. It looked as though whatever took place happened quickly if it makes you feel any better."

Fresh tears welled in the widow's eyes, "It does, and it doesn't, you know? I appreciate you telling me. It appears I don't have as many friends as I thought I did, but it seems I can count you two among them. Thank you." That was all Babette could manage, so Mag and Clara merely nodded before she scurried out the door.

"That was nice of you, Clarie," Mag commented, "And she certainly seems innocent. But you know we've got to make doubly sure."

"I know, Maggie. I know. I think it's time we paid an official visit to Rolling Hills."

Chapter Seven

Mag kept shrewd eyes peeled as Clara maneuvered the old VW bus into the parking lot of the Rolling Hills Country Club, and snapped a mental picture of her surroundings.

The moniker of Rolling Hills fell trite on Mag's ears, but she couldn't deny it a fitting description for the vast expanse of acreage that spanned out against the backdrop of fir trees lining its border.

Mag wondered whether the owner of the neighboring Christmas tree farm had held out for top dollar when the land was sold to make room for all the bored businessmen who considered golf an excellent excuse to get away from the office. And they likely even managed to claim the exorbitant membership fees as a hefty tax write-off.

"Clarie, this bus sticks out like a sore thumb here—I didn't realize so many people in Harmony own a Lexus. Waste of money if you ask me."

"Do me a favor and don't repeat that once we get inside," Clara admonished. "We need to get a good look around, so can you at least pretend to be genuinely interested in joining? I know, it goes against your rebellious nature, but we're not the only innocent suspects in this investigation, so there's more at stake than just our reputations."

Mag put on a fake southern accent and batted her eyelashes at her sister, "Don't forget about my considerable talents as an actress, daahling."

"It's a good thing rich old ladies also tend to come across as eccentric." Clara ignored Mag's blown raspberry, parked the bus, and hurried her sister around a couple of golf carts and through a pair of automatic doors into the main clubhouse.

Mahogany polished to a shine gleamed from every surface as sunlight poured through a wall of windows showcasing a view of the landscaped hills behind the building. Mag noticed a series of tiny flags dotting the expanse as she oriented herself in relation to the crime scene.

A chain link fence separated the clubhouse and its surroundings from the maintenance path that ran alongside Ridge Road. It would serve, Mag assumed, the dual function of keeping patrons confined to approved spaces and deer from wandering freely through the course.

To get from the clubhouse to the spot where Taylor Dean had met his demise would require a lengthy walk to get around the fence, and a detour through sections marked Staff Only.

She waited patiently while Clara spoke to a petite brunette concierge who dripped sweetness and light—

along with a healthy dose of doubt the Balefires could afford the membership fees—while launching into a well-rehearsed sales pitch.

"We have all the amenities you could ask for: golf, of course; tennis; a full-service spa and gym; and a four-star restaurant that caters to our guests' various dietary preferences. And that's not all. Would you ladies like a tour of the facilities? We do offer day passes for potential members if you'd like to explore on your own."

Choosing the latter, Clara scribbled their names into the guest book and handed it to the concierge, who entered them into a sleek, flat-screen computer that beeped a couple of times before a printer housed somewhere beneath the chest-height counter spit out a sheet of visitor's badges.

Mag grimaced as she peeled the label from its paper backing and stuck the offending rectangle right in the center of her tie-dyed tee-shirt which, unfortunately, meant it was positioned over the top of her low-hanging décolletage. Her breasts had been pert once upon a time, but now they bore a striking resemblance to tennis balls in tube socks.

"You can rent a golf cart at the garage out past the spa." The concierge handed over a map and ran a finger over various points of interest. "And if you need equipment or perhaps a new golf or tennis outfit, stop by the pro shop on your way out," She eyed Mag's ensemble with a sidelong glance.

Mag's lips pursed, but to her credit, she refrained from informing the poor girl that there was no way she'd be caught dead in a tennis skirt and, furthermore, she wasn't in the market for a makeover.

Clara peeked into the pro shop on their way back outside, noting that it stocked everything a country clubber might need. Hundreds of loose golf balls filled a four-foot diameter circular bucket in the center of the space, and floor-to-ceiling displays of clubs in various sizes lined the walls, some sporting protective covers that reminded Clara of child-size boxing gloves. Racks of apparel and accessories ranged around the shop, many sporting the Rolling Hills logo in bright colors.

"We're standing right in the center of the club now." Mag opened the map with a flourish the moment they exited the clubhouse, thoroughly enjoying the fact that Clara's annoyingly perky GPS lady was useless for once.

"So, as the crow flies," Mag continued, "the spot of Taylor's demise is due south from here. The golf course takes up the whole northern section, with the clubhouse, spa, and tennis courts acting as a divider."

An efficient layout, Clara supposed.

"Aside from that small, wooded picnic area that stretches down toward the access road where the murder took place, there's not much located on the southwest end. Probably because that road leads into the middle of nowhere." Clara took the words right out of Mag's mouth.

"Exactly, so that access path is for staff, which means those golf cart tracks might not have been left by a guest after all. One of the groundskeepers or even a caddie has more reason to be out here than a member, and since Mayor McCreepy told us the staff has all been cleared, maybe our murderer arrived on foot." Mag suggested.

Clara nodded, rubbing her chin. "It's entirely possible. We need to revisit the scene, but let's check out the steam room first since that's where Babette said she was that morning. As much as my intuition screams she's telling the God's-honest truth, we both know that's not usually the case. Everyone has a secret—I think we learned that from Leanne when Marsha Hutchins was killed. I definitely don't need to see any boudoir photos of Babette Dean, so let's hope hers are a little more PG."

After tugging on the spa door two more times than necessary to figure out that it was locked and required a key card for entry, Clara rolled her eyes and pressed the button marked *guests*.

Another petite brunette staff member buzzed them in and greeted Mag and Clara in a near whisper, even though there were no other guests around to disturb. Dressed the same and similar height and build, this attendant and the one from the main entrance might have been twins.

Like everything else at Rolling Hills, the spa was decorated in tasteful shades of beige and gray that elicited the feeling of complete boredom those of a less adventurous constitution might consider serene. It only made Clara want to go shopping for some colorful throw pillows or at the very least an interesting piece of art to break up the monotony of the neutral tones.

"The spa is through these double doors"—the girl motioned down the hall a bit—"and the women's steam room is on the other side of the locker room down that door to your left. My name is Amy. Let me know if you need any assistance."

"Actually," Clara's eyes twinkled as she tossed a conspiratorial glance at her sister, "A friend of mine recommended I make an appointment with her massage therapist, but I can't remember what she said his name was. Could you check—my friend is Babette Dean, and she was here last Friday morning."

Mag poised herself as backup, ready to let loose a persuasion spell if Amy suddenly proved a model employee. Fortunately, she didn't appear overly concerned with her guests' privacy and agreed to check the schedule if they'd kindly wait a moment.

"Are you sure it was Friday? I don't seem to have an appointment scheduled for your friend that day. I can see she usually books with one of our top therapists, Stefan, though."

Amy tapped on the keys and squinted at the screen, her forehead scrunched together as if she were trying to solve a complicated math problem. "Oh, here it is. Yes, now I remember. Mrs. Dean came in, but canceled her appointment and said she'd rather take a steam. Stefan doesn't have an opening available for the next two days, but I can put you on the list for last-minute cancellations if you'd like."

The idea of being rubbed with fragrant oil for an hour by a masseur named Stefan sounded like a little slice of heaven to Clara, but she tactfully declined, stating she would call around for an appointment next week.

"Maybe they're robot clones," Mag muttered after Amy had taken her leave.

"Maybe you've been binging too much Westworld, Maggie." Clara teased.

Mag rolled her eyes, "No such thing."

The pair marched through a meticulously clean locker room and peeked into the steam room. "There's nobody here right now—and this is just about the same time the murder happened." Clara noticed. "It seems Babette was telling the truth when she said mid-morning is the best time to take a steam—assuming you want to hide your jiggly bits from the rest of the club."

"That woman is a stick. The only way she'd have jiggly bits is if she was covered in Jell-O."

"Ugh, Maggie, I didn't need that mental image," Clara wrinkled her nose.

Ignoring the caution, Mag continued, "Babette definitely came into the spa and canceled her massage. And that clone verified her story that she was in here." She yanked the door open and practically disappeared in the cloud of steam that wafted out.

Mag shook her head and closed the door, "That steam is too much for me. I wouldn't be able to breathe in there for more than two minutes—and that little sign says there's a fifteen-minute maximum. There's no way Babette could have stayed inside that room for an hour. Now, it's getting interesting."

Clara, having begun a thorough search of the changing room during Mag's musings, disappeared around a bank of lockers. "Maggie, come quick. There's another exit back here, marked for employee use."

"I don't see one of those key card contraptions anywhere."

"It's probably only required for entry."

"Let's find out," Mag pushed the metal bar with more force than necessary and stumbled out onto a paved path that surrounded the building and was lined with shrubs and fragrant summer flowers.

Straight ahead, the pavement ended in a dirt path that branched off at right angles. Taking a left would, if Mag's sense of direction was correct, lead straight through a strip of pine trees and down to where Taylor had been murdered.

A lone picnic table squatted on a patch of trampled-down grass about a hundred feet from the exit, next to which sat a plastic cigarette butt disposal container.

Mag pointed to a large rock positioned next to the door they'd just exited. "I'd be willing to bet they use this rock to hold the door open during staff breaks. Which means Babette could have left, whacked her good-for-nothing husband in the side of the head, and slipped back inside without anyone being the wiser."

"Maybe, and if so, she's back on the suspect list. Let's head down to the crime scene, see if it was possible for Babette to have made it there and back." Clara suggested.

Her navigational abilities proved infallible as Mag led Clara past the picnic table, through the woods, and around the fence to where, upon exiting the other side, they approached the same expanse of grass where they'd found the body, except from the opposite angle. "There's no quick way around that fence. Either through the woods or walking along the access path, it's a good ten minutes on foot. Not exactly the speediest of getaways, huh?"

"Not for Babette, or anyone else, unless they were a runner. It's possible, but it seems like a stretch. More likely, the golf cart tracks belong to the killer, just like we thought." Clara held her hands up in a frustrated gesture and pulled Mag along behind her, "We need more information, and I have an idea. Come on."

By the time they'd made it back to the front of the spa, Mag was huffing and puffing and cursing Clara's superior lung capacity. "Where are you taking me?" she snapped

"To the cart garage, for a little subterfuge and petty theft," Clare replied airily, increasing her pace another notch.

Mag grumbled something about not performing magic in public, which Clara, for once, duly ignored. "I swear, Maggie, you'd rather castrate a flock of sheep than agree with me. Sometimes I think you do it just to grate on my last nerve! And I never said anything about performing magic, but you know what? You've convinced me to do just that."

"Oh, and I'm the petulant, combative sister?" Mag shook her head, a wide smile spreading across her face, "Then again, maybe I just push it because you're the most fun when you're acting like a rebel. You should do it more often."

Clara shot her a sideways glance. "And perhaps you should do it less frequently. Then I wouldn't have to be the level-headed one all the time. Do you really think I give a unicorn fart about what Penelope Starr thinks? Oh, to Hades with it." Clara let out a grunt, took a furtive look around, and muttered a spell under her breath.

"Technically," She qualified, "We're not in public." And with the whisper of a breath, the golf cart sign-out sheet appeared in her hand.

"Risky, conjuring like that." Mag commented, her voice holding a measure of pride.

"Says here, the only people with golf carts signed out that morning were Miriam May, Maude Prescott, Perry Weatherall, and Selena Sanderson." Clara read.

Mag's nose crinkled, "Now why does that last name sound familiar?"

"Because she's a member of our coven. Good Goddess, Maggie, what happened to your memory anyway? Do I need to start growing some ginkgo biloba in the backyard?" Clara retorted, exasperated.

"So which one screams *murderer* to you? I refuse to finger Perry Weatherall for another murder after last time, and I don't think we've met anyone named Miriam." Mag argued.

"You haven't, but I've met her at book club." Clara retorted. "She's the one who picked the book this month. Maude said Miriam ended up with her cart, and you'd know the girl from the coven if you saw her. She's part of that contingent of young witches who don't know their brooms from a hole in the ground. But nice enough."

"Young equals capable, but again, why?" Mag asked.

"I have no idea, but at least we know more than we did before we came here. Come on, let's get back to the VW and find ourselves some lunch."

Chapter Eight

"Funny, isn't it, how it always seems to be the most intriguing and complicated people who get murdered. Of course, those very qualities often speak to motive in the first place. First Marsha, whose voracious curiosity helped her stumble upon information that had long been buried, and now Taylor, who managed to inspire a variety of conflicting assumptions about his character."

Clara knew when Mag became philosophical, it meant she was deep in investigative mode.

"And it all comes down to motive, doesn't it?" A rhetorical question, so Clara maneuvered the VW bus back to Harmony's town center and continued to maintain her silence while her sister worked through the tangled web of clues and impressions they'd gathered so far.

"Mail tampering and theft, that's all we've got—and really, I'm surprised we know this much considering we've only lived in town for a few months. Taylor's been a mail carrier for years; he's probably stolen from half the town. Doesn't exactly narrow down our suspect pool.

Which means we have to do something I really don't want to do."

"What's that?" Clara asked with trepidation.

"Be sociable and see what else we can dig up. Speaking of which, pull over in front of the post office. We still haven't received our fruit of the month basket, and I intend to lodge a complaint. I was quite looking forward to the figs and Tosca pears from Italy. It's a treat to get them this early in the season."

Clara did as she was instructed, and followed Mag inside the post office, where she demanded to speak to the postmaster who, even though the two-hour lunch break had long ago ended, had to be called away from his turkey sandwich.

He didn't look pleased when he realized the interruption involved placating an irritated old woman but brightened considerably at Clara's megawatt smile.

Affably pleasant, he was attractive enough, she supposed. His hazel eyes looked slightly magnified by a pair of round, wire-framed glasses, but their expression remained warm and friendly.

A feat, considering his job probably came with plenty of dealing-with-the-public angst. If she'd been in the mood for a man, he might do nicely.

"As I said, the shipment wasn't insured, so my hands are tied, but if you contact the vendor and explain what happened, it's possible you'll get a credit, or they might reship." The postmaster apologized. "You've probably heard we lost our mail carrier, which is no excuse, but we're short-handed at the moment."

"Thank you for taking the time to look into it, and we're sorry for your loss. We're new in town, so we didn't know Taylor except as our mail carrier." Clara pasted on a sympathetic smile.

"It's his poor wife who'll feel it the most. Taylor took real good care of that woman, and it wasn't just because she's delicate. I can't imagine what she'll do now. Anyhow, life goes on, so they say."

"They certainly do," Clara replied. "You know we saw Mr. Dean on the day of the murder. Not too long before it happened." She showed him her sympathetic face but kept her eyes trained on his to gauge his response.

"No, I wasn't aware of that." Nothing there but sorrow.

"He was talking to Reggie Blackthorne, and it looked like they might have been arguing, but we've heard Reggie isn't considered a suspect."

"Oh, I can tell you what that was all about. Reggie was hot-dogging up the dirt road in that truck of his and kicked up a good-sized stone. Cracked the side window of the mail truck. Taylor called me with the news as soon as Reggie left. I was the last person to speak to him before he died."

The misery on his face caused Clara to reach out and squeeze his hand. That and a genuine smile turned his thoughts away from the pain of Taylor's death.

"I can't offer you exotic fruits, but if you'd give me your number, I'd love to take you to dinner sometime." His hopeful smile only made him more attractive, but

Clara regretfully declined. To her way of thinking, this was not the time for romance.

"Why did you do that, Clarie?" Mag burst out as soon as the door swung shut behind her.

"Do what?"

"Brush him off like that. He was the sexiest postmaster I've ever seen. What gives?"

"Hecate's petticoats, Maggie, you're still the boy-crazy teenager I used to share a bedroom with, aren't you?"

"In my defense, you were always a bit of a prude, so I had to make up for the both of us. I thought you'd outgrown that, but apparently not."

Clara sighed, "And in mine, you have always mistaken my unwillingness to settle as a character flaw. It took me two hundred years to find a man I wanted to make babies with, and it didn't exactly turn out to be all sunshine and roses. Pardon me if I don't feel like spending the next fifty-odd years filled with pain and regret."

She left out the phrase *like I've spent the last fifty*, but both she and Mag knew it was implied.

"He asked you out to dinner, not for your hand in marriage. A little perspective might be in order. A date wouldn't hurt you." *And a roll in the hay might smooth out your nerves*—Mag kept the last to herself since ticking off her sister wasn't the goal.

"Not happening." Clenched teeth flattened the words a bit.

Mag held up her hands. "It's your business. I'll stay out of it." She closed her mouth and kept it locked tight. She was treading into dangerous territory and knew when to wave the white flag.

Or not.

She pushed anyway. "Fine, if you want to drag your emotional baggage around, who am I to judge? But you're living like you're still stuck in stone, watching the world go by."

"That might be the meanest thing you've ever said to me. Do you have any idea how hard it was to watch my granddaughter grow up thinking her mother and grandmother had murdered each other? Knowing I couldn't kiss and make it better if she fell, or guide her in the ways of our kind? Even arms made from dead stone ache with emptiness."

"Then why? Why are you shutting yourself away from life again?"

While Clara considered herself openly honest and could count empathy as one of her greatest strengths, confronting her own hangups was just as difficult for her as anyone else.

She heaved a sigh, and Mag could sense the sadness behind it. "I failed so miserably with my daughter and again with my granddaughter, though for different reasons."

"You didn't," Mag insisted. "Sylvana's not dead and you visit Lexi every other day."

"You don't understand. No witch has ever come back from a total stoning to tell the tale. I had no idea, still don't come to that, if being awake and aware is part of the punishment. I thought Sylvana dead by my hand."

"The whole time?" A consideration Mag hadn't thought of before. "But she wasn't and it's all over now."

"Not entirely. I meant to stop her at any cost. I would have killed her if that was what it took." Admitting one of her deepest secrets left Clara feeling vulnerable.

"Then you're paying penance by not going to dinner with the nice man?"

Clara was done with the conversation. "Get your head out of your hormones. Better yet, get it out of mine," she snapped.

"Maybe you should have asked for a hair shirt and a good flogging for your birthday."

Clara's burning look of response carried just enough magic to set the tips of Mag's fingers tingling.

She flapped her hand, dismissing Clara's concerns. "Lexi's fine. She had a bit of a bump in her emotional road is all. But she came through it like a Balefire, with flair if not dignity or grace. We pop over to Port Harbor at least three times a week, and this is the last time you can trot out that tired excuse for why you're holding back. But I'm sorry if I hurt your feelings." For Mag, the admission came with difficulty.

"It's okay, water under the bridge. You might as well head on home. I'll walk back after my book club meeting which, as it happens, starts in fifteen minutes."

Somewhere along the line, Clara had learned to shut down her emotions—learned to live in that numb place between pleasure and pain—and though she was sure it would happen at some point, she wasn't quite ready for romantic feelings to bubble their way back up to the surface. Grateful that her sister let it go this time, Clara sent up a silent thank you to the Goddess and vowed to try and be more open to the conversation next time Mag brought it up.

Mag watched her sister in the rear-view mirror as she pulled away and made a vow of her own: to ferret out whatever haunted Clara and expose the specter to the light of truth. Because Mag would bet her best spell, it had nothing to do with Lexi or Sylvana.

With no idea her past was about to become Mag's new obsession, Clara strolled down the sidewalk and made an effort to shrug off the difficult conversation.

Meandering down the sidewalk in the middle of her reverie, Clara failed to see Angela Sinclair, who in typical New England small-town fashion, bustled over to say hello.

"Hi there, remember me? I was in your shop the other morning. That face cream of yours is amazing. My cheeks feel like a baby's bottom."

It took a second for Clara to place Angela, but when she did it all came flooding back. Her promise to attend a garden club meeting that was curtailed by the discovery of a dead body.

"Hi Angela, of course, I remember you." Clara offered a convincing smile. "I'm glad you're enjoying the cream, and I intended to make it to your garden club but, well, things have been a bit hectic lately. How are you all doing with the hummingbird problem?"

She knew darned well they hadn't been able to banish the little beasts and hoped the pixies were laying low enough to escape discovery until she and Mag managed to figure out how to convince Hagatha to return them to the Faelands.

Angela explained that the ornithological association still hadn't returned the garden club's phone call, setting Clara's mind at ease for the time being. After a few more pleasantries, the woman bade her goodbye and headed on down Main Street, leaving her to her own thoughts.

The scent of freshly brewed coffee wafted out of the window of Evelyn's bakery and, combined with that of the lightest, airiest yeast donuts in existence, set Clara's mouth to watering. While she was waiting for her splurge order of a large iced caramel macchiato, she spotted Leanne Snow at a window seat, furiously scanning her copy of Fifty Shades of Grey in preparation for book club.

"Hey, Leanne, are you enjoying the book?" Clara asked with a grin and slid into the seat across the table.

Fresh-faced now that she'd given up her habit of plastering on a mask of makeup, Leanne looked at least a decade younger than she had a couple of months before. One benefit, Clara supposed, of a near-death experience is learning what's most important in life, and Leanne certainly seemed different after hers.

Disgusted, Leanne threw the book down on the table between them, "To be perfectly honest, BDSM doesn't really light my fire the way it seems to do for everyone else. But forget about book club, how are you doing?"

Pausing to take a bite of sugary, fried perfection, Clara wondered what Leanne would say if she gave her a perfectly honest answer. Since any such insight would contain more than a kernel of her magical truth, Clara concentrated on recent events only.

"All right. Though I have to say, it's more than a little disconcerting to have discovered two dead bodies since moving to town."

Leanne's mouth dropped open in surprise, "You found Taylor Dean's body? How did I miss out on that detail? I was there, you know. At the club that day, I mean." She shuddered. "While it was happening."

A happy coincidence. Clara thought and capitalized on the opportunity placed in her path and pumped Leanne for details.

"Did you see anything?"

Leanne put down her coffee, picked up a paper napkin, and began to tear it into shreds. "I've gone over and over it in my mind in case there was some detail I missed, but no. I saw nothing out of the ordinary."

"You know the police are looking at Babette for this, right? Do you think she's capable of murder?"

"If you asked me six months ago, I'd have said no one in this town was capable of murder, but we both know how wrong I would have been." Leanne raised one eyebrow and studied Clara's face, "And no, I didn't know she was the prime suspect."

Thinking, Leanne paused, and a second napkin turned to confetti between her fingers before she answered. "Not Babette. It doesn't play for me at all. The cops are way off base."

"I think so, too. Who do you think might have had a motive?"

"You're investigating again, aren't you? Okay, here's what I know: Babette couldn't have done it. Not unless she's hiding some serious skills. She'd have to be a magician, or a witch, or something."

Clara jolted at the word witch, and then forced herself to think of the gravity of the situation to keep a smile from sliding across her lips, "And why is that?"

"She was at the spa the whole time. I know because I watched her go in after I helped her pick up the scattered contents of her purse. She'd dropped it while trying to find her key card, and stuff was strewn all over the place. Did you know she carries an entire medicine cabinet around with her? Everything from bandages to some pretty potent painkillers. The woman is a menace to polite society, but not because she's a killer; she's a klutz."

Having seen Babette in action, Clara nodded her agreement and took another bite of donut.

"That's what she told the police—that she was in the steam room at the time of the murder. Staff confirm she went in, but Ma—my mother and I—checked it out, and she could have gone out the back exit, jumped in a handy golf cart, killed Taylor, and then slipped back in."

"Not possible. You see, right after I talked to Babette, I got a text saying my tennis lesson was canceled, and since it was such a nice day, I walked through the gardens and sat at that little picnic table near that back door. I had just picked this up"—Leanne indicated the copy of Fifty Shades still lying on the table—"and I figured I'd get a head start before my massage."

Leanne tilted her head slightly, looking up while she pulled the scene out of her memory. "She'd have had to go right past me, and nobody did. Not on foot or in a golf cart."

"If you saw her there, why didn't you tell the police?" One word would have put an end to that line of questioning and saved Babette days of panic and heartache.

"They never asked, but that's probably because nobody knew I was there. I forgot my key card and never checked in at the front desk. Missed my massage, but I was sitting in plain sight of the back door while Taylor Dean got himself killed not a mile away."

Another shudder rippled down Leanne's body, but all Clara could think about was the fact that apparently, the security at Rolling Hills was lax enough that people could come and go without notice.

"I left before the police arrived at the club, and before you ask, I heard the sirens, but there's a speed trap just the other side of the main exit." She lifted a shoulder. "People get pulled over all the time, so I didn't think anything of it. I heard the news when I got back here, but it never occurred to me that I might know anything valuable."

Making a mental note to warn her lead-footed sister about the speed trap, Clara offered Leanne a sage piece of advice.

"You really should speak to Chief Cobb, or maybe call that nice young detective, Lynn Nye. Get them off Babette's scent before the poor woman keels over from a heart attack. Though, what she could have been doing in the steam room for an hour is beyond me."

"That I can't speak to, but I will talk to the police, Clara. As soon as book club is over, I promise. Now, tell me how this thing ends so I don't look like the biggest prude in Harmony."

Clara wondered why that word kept coming up in conversation and lamented the fact that an unwillingness to give it up to every Tom, Dick, and Harry was considered a character flaw in this day and age. Most particularly by her own sister.

Book club, Clara discovered when she arrived, had divided itself into three camps. The progressive group who had lobbied hard to add such a titillating book to the roster squared off against the opposition who pressed their lips together and glared. And then there were the leftovers who preferred to hide their true feelings under a discussion of symbolism and pretension.

Spearheading the first group was Miriam May, a buxom brunette with a less-is-more philosophy when it came to clothes. In her case, however, less wasn't nearly enough to provide adequate coverage in all areas. A fact

Clara learned when Miriam bent over to retrieve a dropped pen and flashed half an inch of rear cleavage below a beautifully inked tattoo.

Chapter Nine

While Clara turned to the type of solace some women seek when they're stressed out—scrubbing and dusting every surface in the shop, sans magic—Mag ensconced herself in the back room alchemy lab in an attempt to thwart Hagatha's pixie plot once and for all.

With Leanne having removed the last vestiges of suspicion from Babette Dean, they were no closer to solving the murder, and the thought of being the subjects of an investigation was more than a little disconcerting.

After several bangs followed by what would have been a string of profanities if not for the anti-cussing charm old Haggie placed on the house, Mag stomped back through the connecting door, leaving a sticky trail behind her.

"Honestly, I think that woman believes she was the inspiration for the character of Hagrid. Next thing you know, she'll be hatching up a dragon's egg, and the whole town will be burnt to cinders. Those pixies are kind of cute though. I have to give her that."

"What exactly did you do to the poor thing?"

"Really, Clarie?" Exasperated, Mag shook her head. "I didn't hurt her. I just tried to get her to talk, but I think she signed a Pentagon-level non-disclosure agreement, and she won't budge."

Mag paced the room and ran a crooked finger over the aged patina of a Pennsylvania Dutch porch bench before stopping in front of the writing box Taylor Dean stole from her.

"You'd think after all my years, the depravity of humanity wouldn't bother me anymore. Especially considering the things I've seen people do to one another. This guy was clearly not one of the *good guys* if such a thing can be quantified, but his crimes were too petty for someone to want to murder him. Seems like he kept his indiscretions a secret from his poor wife."

Clara watched her sister's face go blank, then frowned as Mag ran her hands over the writing box. Mag let out a low whistle and bustled into the back room to return with a paper clip.

"What are you going to do with that?"

"Writing boxes of this era almost always have a secret compartment for hiding sensitive documents. With everything going on, I'd forgotten to check before, and I just found the hidden latch on this one. It's spring-loaded, so I can use the paper clip to pop it open." Since it was early in the morning and no one was in the shop to see her do it, Mag conjured an over-sized magnifying glass from her cottage in the backyard.

Bending the paper clip open, Mag gently thrust the tip into a hole that looked like part of the wood grain. She gave the tool a wiggle, then a jiggle, pulled it out and tried again.

"Just got to get the right angle, and then a little push." Clara leaned in for a better look.

A soft click sounded from inside the box, and with delight in her eyes, Mag let out a cackle worthy of the wicked witch of the West. Using her fingernail, she eased the hidden drawer from the space.

"Jackpot," Mag declared triumphantly, waving a tattered manila envelope in the air. "Probably a bunch of old receipts, but you never know. Could be letters from some historical figure and worth a bundle."

But when she opened the envelope, it turned out she could not have been more wrong. A handful of modern photographs and a small notebook tumbled out onto the counter.

Clara crowed in for a peek at the first picture, "And you said you didn't want to see any more x-rated photos. The girls in my book club would love these. Speaking of which, I recognize that woman."

"Which one?" Mag exclaimed. "And how? All you can see is her backside."

"Trust me, it's Miriam May. Unless there are two women in town with the same butterfly tattoo. Thing is, that's not Gregory, the man she introduced as her husband when he picked her up last time."

Miriam's husband had dark, curly hair, a rather prominent nose, and wore his eyebrows plucked into a feminine-looking arch. The man with his face buried between Miriam's breasts was blond, and his eyebrows—that was all Clara could see if his face—had never known the touch of a tweezer.

Mag tsked. "It just gets more and more interesting, doesn't it? Taylor Dean was a pervert and a peeping Pete."

"You mean Tom," Clara corrected.

"Whatever. What do you want to bet he was blackmailing her?" Mag retorted before flipping to the next photo in the stack and letting out a low whistle. "Ding, ding, ding. Got his face in this one and you'll never guess who it is." She waved the photo in front of Clara's face.

"It can't be!" Snatching the photo, Clara took a closer look. "Well, I'll be a hot cauldron on a cold day. That's our neighbor, Leonard Wayland, getting a piece of Mrs. May. They're having an affair." Scandalized, Clara almost whispered.

"And the mailman knew about it, so we finally have a solid lead." Mag flipped through the rest of the short stack of photos. "Mrs. May certainly is limber."

"I'd give her a 9.3 if she can stick the landing."

"Eww." Grossing out Mag took effort, but every so often, Clara managed to zing one in under the radar.

"This explains the conversation between Leonard and Taylor that day on the street. I thought their encounter smelled a little like rotten tuna." Mag's brow furrowed at the memory.

"Don't say tuna too loud; you'll have Jinx begging for sushi," Clara warned. "And let's not forget, Miriam

May checked out a golf cart the day of the murder. Leonard Wayland isn't the only one with something to lose, and he has an airtight alibi."

"It could just as easily been Miriam who did the deed, I agree." Putting down the photos, Mag picked up the palm-sized spiral bound notebook and flipped it open.

"Huh. I thought there'd be something interesting, but it's blank." She slid it across to Clara. "What a letdown."

Pointing to the torn edge of a sheet caught in the wire binding, Clara said, "I wonder if—" And without another word, she dashed into the back room and returned with a glowing cinder cradled in the palm of her hand. The air chilled a few degrees and gusts of frosty mist billowed from her lips as she blew on it until the piece of charcoal was cold enough to use.

With gentle care, she slid the inky chunk over the paper with just enough force to leave a bit of residue behind.

"It's working." Clara chortled as the words began to appear. "It's a list of names. Miriam and Leonard are on there, but it looks like they were crossed out. Same with their spouses, and these two are unreadable, but look what we have here."

"Reggie Blackthorne." Mag pounded her fist against the countertop.

"Looks like he had more going with Taylor than cracking a window with the tribute-to-testosterone truck. Blackmail is a good motive for murder."

"Convenient, too, given he was there the day of the murder. Cops ruled him out, but that's no guarantee he's innocent. I wonder what Taylor had on him. Does it say anything else? Try another page, maybe there are more details."

There weren't. Only the name.

"I'm just telling you now, if I have to see naked pictures of him, I want you to be ready with a memory charm." A delicate shudder made Clara's shoulders twitch.

"Who do you want to investigate first?"

While she thought about it, Mag flipped the sign from Closed to Open and unlocked the shop door with a sense of anticipation. Surly as she might seem, the art of the haggle set her juices flowing. Not as much as investigating a murder, but enough to look forward to the day.

"Flip a coin." She meant to say it didn't matter to her but focused instead on the familiar figure moving toward the shop. "Nix the murder talk and get those photos under wraps, here comes the fuzz."

"Honestly, Mag, no one has used that term since the early eighties," but Clara slid the envelope under the counter as Chester Cobb and his faithful sidekick pushed open the door.

Chapter Ten

As if it were second nature, Cobb scanned the shop on entry, his flat gaze taking in the contents without giving away an iota of reaction. In response, Clara maintained her unflappable cool and welcomed the pair with the offer of a pitcher of freshly squeezed lemonade. The chief declined, but young Deputy Nye accepted a glass. Her cop-stare would need a few years of seasoning before it reached any level of intimidation, Clara decided.

"It has come to our attention that you had a vendetta against Taylor Dean." Chief Cobb seemed to have grown a pair since the last Harmony murder and didn't bother beating around the bush.

Mag pierced the chief with a glare that could have sliced in half a four-foot-wide ice sculpture, and put on her loftiest tone. "The same could be said for any of the unfortunate souls who were cursed to have been included on his delivery route."

Cobb's chagrined expression told Mag he had, indeed, also been a victim of the mailman's negligence, though he declined to trash talk the victim. A point in his favor as far as she was concerned, but Mag would always press against the boundaries.

"Then again, if doing a lousy job was a solid motive for murder, you'd be knee-deep in dead bodies any given day of the week." More nimble than she looked, Mag avoided the kick Clara sent toward her shins and moved farther down the length of the counter just as the bell over the door signaled another shopper entering the store.

"Is the offer still open for that greenhouse tour? I've a hankering to whip up some herbal seasoning blends, and I wanted to see what you have in stock." Maude Prescott had no idea how bad her timing was.

"Go ahead, Ms. Balefire." Cobb irritated Clara by dismissing her in her own store. "I'll speak with your mother first."

"It's fine, Clarie. Don't you worry about a thing." Mag never took her eyes off the chief of police when she said it, which did nothing to reassure her sister. But it seemed she had no other choice.

As Maude followed Clara out the back, they heard the chief's voice harden. "Mr. Dean's job performance is not the issue here, and it certainly isn't justification for his death. You sound quite bitter, Ms. Balefire, and you were at the scene of the crime. If you're trying to further implicate yourself, you're succeeding."

Torn between the need to get Maude out of earshot and staying where she was needed, Clara made a choice and called upon her magic. Power rippled out from her center, through the alchemy lab/storage room, and out into the backyard.

Cauldrons shimmered and turned into cardboard boxes, the balefire went from flames of cheerful pink to traditional orange. Exotic plantings faded behind an impenetrable glamour in both greenhouse and gardens.

"Just through the back door, Maude, feel free to start without me, and I'll join you shortly." That crisis handled, Clara shot Mag a pointed look, silently willing her sister to shut her blasted mouth for once in her life.

"First poor Babette, and now me. I won't pretend to have liked the man, but killing someone because he didn't properly deliver my mail is a little over the top. Do I look capable of taking down a man half again my size?" Cane tapping on the floor, Mag rounded the end of the sales counter and went toe to toe with Chief Cobb.

The top of her head came roughly to the lower line of his shirt pocket, and her posture seemed even more hunched over when she cocked her head to look up at him. Anyone looking at the pair of them would find the notion laughable. Unless they were familiar with Mag's work, and then, maybe not so much.

"Mrs. Dean has established an ironclad alibi." Officer Nye spoke up for the first time and earned herself a quelling glance from her superior for airing police business in front of a suspect. Leanne must have come through. Good for her.

Declining to comment on her physicality, Cobb stated, "There are many motives for murder, but I wouldn't be a very good cop if I didn't question the person who had an altercation with the victim less than twenty-four hours prior to his death, now would I?"

Knowing that if she said anything, it would come out as a snide comment about what it would take to make Chester Cobb a good cop, Mag sucked back the retort and merely pierced him with another withering glare.

"Now, with all due respect, Chief Cobb, my mother is clearly an ailing, elderly woman, and it's highly unlikely that she could have inflicted the amount of damage done to Taylor Dean. If you had any actual evidence to that end, you'd be cuffing her and reading her rights by now." Clara's voice dripped honey but carried the ability to sting like a bee.

Lynn Nye emitted a noise that could have been construed as a cough to a less discerning ear.

"Maybe not, but you look quite capable to me, and as far as I'm concerned, you two are a package deal." It was Clara's turn in the hot seat.

"Maybe so, but unless you intend to arrest one of us, I think we've already told you everything we know." Mag shot a pointed look at the door and stood in stony silence while Clara ushered the pair toward the door.

"Please call us if you think of anything else, and don't—"

"Leave town. Yeah, we know the drill." Clara finished Lynn's sentence for her, but there was no malice in her tone. She had nothing against the young cop, even if she had a boob for a partner.

"Don't talk to me right now," she directed at Mag after she closed the door behind them. She brushed past her sister on the way to join Maude in the greenhouse. "You made it worse. Develop some people skills."

Just outside the door, Clara paused, closed her eyes, inhaled and exhaled rhythmically until the rant bubbling up in her throat drifted away. Mag tried her patience like no one else.

Centered and calm again, she lifted her chin, plastered on a smile that only felt a little bit fake, and sailed out into the garden to find Maude hastily striding away down the mulched path.

"Is this sweet cicely?" A little out of breath, the older woman ran a gentle finger of the fern-like fronds and bent to sniff the cluster of white blooms. "Myrrhis odorata. Sweet to the taste, with a hint of licorice flavor. Great in medicinal teas for the digestion, but even better in apple pie. Would you be willing to sell a cutting?"

At this point, Clara would give her a handful of them if it got Maude out of her hair, so she could go back in and deal with the fallout from Chief Cobb's visit.

"Of course, let me—"

"Oh, no need," Maude assured and pulled a pair of scissors out of the woven bag she carried for a purse. "I'm always prepared for such occasions." Clara put the avid gleam in her eye down to gardener's greed.

It took almost an hour before Maude settled up her bill and toddled off with a purse stuffed full of fragrant greenery, leaving Clara feeling like a fleeced sheep.

Mag, denied the benefit of a head-clearing walk through the garden, was doing her best to pace a rut in the floor behind the sales counter when Clara returned. Cheap shoes applied at speed to the carpet had turned her already fuzzy hairdo into a static-laden halo above her pink scalp.

"I swear to Circe, I'm going to turn that man into a toad one of these days. No, not a toad, a flea. Actually, a male praying mantis. It'll be fun to watch his head get bitten off—literally."

"And you wonder why he thinks you might be responsible. Come on, Maggie, can't you at least try to fit in? We're supposed to be blending in here. Wasn't that the point? Keep to ourselves, tone down the magic, maintain the status quo?"

To give her mind an outlet, Clara retrieved a basket of fragrant dried herbs and a handful of paper cones to make potpourri sachets while Mag ranted and paced.

"What if I don't *want* to maintain the status quo, Clarie?" Mag's eyebrows scrunched together as she griped on. "I told you there was a seedy underbelly. No wonder, a name like Harmony. Sounds innocuous, but of course nothing is ever as it seems."

The rant continued. Hagatha had the right of it, to Mag's way of thinking. The witches in this town were a bunch of snivelers. They'd abandoned the ways of their mothers before them, and were a disgrace to all witchkind.

Clara's only outward response to her sister's display of temper was to twist the top of each cone with more force until she finally overstepped the boundaries of the paper and popped the top right off of one. Potpourri flew, and she tossed the torn cone back into the basket and swept the crumbs off the counter.

Head tilted, Clara waited until the steam had stopped pouring from Mag's ears before allowing herself to speak.

"Are you done, now that you've descended to your unhappy place? You're not even speaking in complete sentences anymore. Get it together, Maggie! You cannot keep tap dancing on Chief Cobb's last nerve, whether you like him or not. To be perfectly honest, I'm getting tired of being the only one of us capable of keeping a level head."

Just as Clara had expected, Mag's surly mood deflated, and after a few deep breaths, she had nearly returned to what passed for balanced.

"I'm sorry, Clarie. Really. I don't want to make things any harder on you than they already are. You have to understand that I'm simply not capable of keeping my nose out of things—especially not when there's an innocent on the line. It's just part of who I am. If that puts me in the line of fire, it's my version of normal."

"And I love who you are. I would just prefer not to have to memory charm everyone in town—particularly not the police. Rides the fine edge of our oath to cause no harm." Elbow leaning on the counter, Clara held up a finger, "And don't bother trotting out the *it's for the greater good* excuse because I'm not buying. Not in this case, anyway."

Mag's tone turned to one of determination, "Then we need to solve this murder post-haste, pardon the pun, so that I can get that man off my back once and for all."

"The naughty couple. I say we tail Mrs. May, insert ourselves into a situation where we can gather information, and find some proof. You game?" Mag asked, a mischievous twinkle in her eye.

"You know I am. Jinx! Pye! Wake your lazy tails up." Clara's shout was followed by a yowl that turned into a yawn as the pitter-patter of paws on stairs turned to heavy footsteps when both familiars took human form to answer their master's command.

Pye turned wide eyes on Clara, and geared up for a major guilt trip, "I didn't realize we were going to be used for slave labor when you proposed the plan to open this place." Pye grumbled.

"I'm guessing our mailman didn't realize he was going to be whacked to death with a golf club when he signed on for the job, either." Clara admonished, though she couldn't really blame Pyewacket for being annoyed. "And if we don't figure out who did the whacking, your next assignment will be breaking us out of jail. I promise, once this is over we'll take a little trip upstate to that stream with the salmon you like, and we'll let the magics flow free."

All Mag had to do was cast a narrow-eyed sidelong glance at Jinx, who swallowed his protests while focusing on the prospect of fresh fish and a chance to practice more spellwork. She beckoned Clara to the back room, then pulled a Harmony town map and a pendulum from a supply drawer and prepared to scry.

"Like to see you use that GSP app thing for this," she crowed.

"GPS." Clara corrected, then flicked a finger and the cloth covering the round table whisked into the air to reveal a pentacle etched into the surface. Inlaid with Living Gold, a material forged by the gods, the five-pointed star would act as a magical conduit.

She placed a white candle at each spot where the surrounding circle intersected with the star's points, lighting each one while calling on the elements of earth, air, fire, water, and spirit.

When the air began to vibrate with magical energy, Mag placed the map in the center of the pentacle, dangling the pendulum over it by the tip of its silver chain.

"Show me the location of Miriam May." At Mag's command, the rose-quartz crystal spun around, its point finally touching down on the spot where the country club was located.

"She's at Rolling Hills," Mag said, her eyes gleaming. "How convenient is that? Returning to the scene of the crime. What do you say, Clarie? I think we should take the chance on a skim."

Clara agreed driving the bus would take too much time, and agreed to use the witchy ability to teleport from place to place instead. "We can land in the woods behind the clubhouse. Let's go."

In the blink of an eye, Pye and Jinx were left alone in the shop, while their masters appeared out of thin air beneath the cover of a thick section of pines.

Chapter Eleven

"Oomph! What happened?" Clara gasped with what was left of her breath. Flat on her back after a rare tuck-and-roll landing, she blinked up at the sky. "That cloud looks like a narwhal if you squint a little."

"Did you hit your head?" Using her cane for balance, Mag struggled to her feet. "Sorry about the rough touchdown. Minor miscalculation on my part."

So rarely did Mag misjudge a landing, Clara didn't have the heart to tease. Much. "I'm fine," she said. "What did you do? Jig sideways to avoid a moose?"

"This close to the club? Hardly. I didn't remember this hill being quite so steep, and I lost my footing when we touched down."

"The leg?" Concern replaced levity when Clara tried to lift her sister's skirts to check.

"Get off me, Clara. I mean it. I'm fine. Now let's get this done." Dusting herself off, Mag took off down the hill.

"You're going the wrong way." Clara, phone in hand and keyed up to the GPS app, called out.

Reversing, Mag shot her nose in the air and marched past her sister in as fine a huff as Clara had ever seen. According to the club's website, Wednesdays were reserved for poolside classes, and that gave Clara an idea.

"Limp a little harder," she suggested when she caught up with Mag at the edge of the last strand of trees and stepped onto the trimmed grass bordering the fairway.

"Excuse me?" Mag looked ready to throw down on the spot if she even suspected Clara meant to insult.

"I mean, make like you need that cane even more than you do already because we're enrolling you in water aerobics with the cover that it's part of your physical therapy. Miriam mentioned she takes this class, so I think that's our best bet." Clara waited for the inevitable blowup, but it never came. She was beginning to wonder if her sister had mellowed, but decided not to hold her breath.

"I'm going to need regular therapy after spending an afternoon as a water ballerina, but if it helps us catch a murderer, I suppose it's a small price to pay."

"That's the spirit. Now hustle. It starts in five." Clara started for the spa and had taken a handful of steps before she realized Mag wasn't on her heels.

Instead, she'd slid behind the wheel of a golf cart conveniently abandoned alongside a nearby maintenance shed and was now cocking an eyebrow at Clara, who rolled her eyes and climbed into what she hoped wasn't going to turn into a death machine.

Pedal to the metal, they rolled into the club parking lot in under ninety seconds. "Thanks for the hairstyle, Maggie. I look like the bride of Frankenstein."

Getting around the front desk attendant required a white lie and a whiff of magic to reactivate their guest credentials. If Clara felt a hint of remorse for contravening her coven's magical lockdown decree, she pushed it down deep. It was already too late for that, and if bringing a killer to justice required breaking rules that never should have been made in the first place, who were they hurting?

With a clear conscience, she weaved through the maze of hallways to the pool-adjacent ladies' locker room and realized they were in danger of being late after all.

Popping into the privacy of adjoining stalls, the Balefire sisters threw caution down the toilet and magicked themselves into bathing attire. Clara sported a black-and-white polka-dotted maillot that made her look like a brunette Veronica Lake, while Mag conjured some striped relic from the turn of the century that resembled a potato sack with straps.

"You cannot go in there wearing that." Clara took a surreptitious look around and then transformed her sister's outfit into something country-club worthy, if not entirely fashionable. "There, let's go. Thank the Goddess none of the coven members are here right now. We've broken the *no magic in public* rule about a half-dozen times already today."

"I refute that rule," Mag scowled but followed Clara to the pool. "Are you sure this is a good idea?" She picked at the rear of her suit, pulling it into a more comfortable position. "My lady parts are—"

Clara pinched the bridge of her nose. "I beg of you, do not finish that sentence. Now, get in the water and aerobicize yourself or whatever." Clara sniffed at the sharp scent of chlorinated water and spent a passing thought on the way the humidity was going to affect her hair while she scanned the room for her quarry.

Not only were Lydia Wayland and Miriam May both in attendance, they sported nearly matching swimsuits and were huddled together, giggling like the best of girlfriends.

With all the tender mercy of a drill sergeant, the instructor divided the class into two groups. Mag landed in the beginner/special needs category while Clara jockeyed for position and congratulated herself for ending up next to Lydia.

But that was the last bit of joy she experienced as she learned that, in the advanced group, a person could sweat while surrounded by cool water.

With three feet of water providing plenty of resistance, Clara sidestepped around the perimeter of the designated area with Lydia on one side and Miriam on the other. Her breathing increased to short gasps as the women crowded close and urged her to move faster.

The one time she chanced a look at Mag, she saw her sister gliding through the exercises with ease. Sometimes life wasn't fair.

"Move it or lose it, Balefire." Barely a whisper over five feet tall, the instructor proved the cliché about dynamite and small packages. Her muscles had muscles on them, Clara thought as she stepped up her pace. All her plans for engaging Lydia and Miriam in conversation flew into the chlorinated mist rising off the surface of the pool.

"I'm out of shape," she finally gasped when they stopped moving sideways and started a series of knee lifts. Not the greatest conversation opener, but she went with it.

"Oh, honey, this is only the warm-up." Lydia shot Clara an endorphin-laced grin. Madness. "We're just getting started."

"I'm going to die in this pool." Mag would have to carry on the Balefire name without her.

"At least it won't be murder. We've had enough of those to last a lifetime." Lydia turned her attention back to Miriam, leaving Clara to parse her tone for remorseful subtext. Finding none, she back-burnered thoughts of murder and concentrated only on surviving the exercise in water torture. Or water torture of exercise. Either description seemed appropriate.

When it was over, Mag climbed out of the pool feeling limber and energized while Clara eyed the ladder with dread and wondered if she could lift her leg high enough to step onto the first rung.

"Get out up here before they get away." Leaning over the edge, Mag hissed at Clara, looked back over her shoulder, and took matters into her own hands. Moving faster than she had in years, she hit the locker room just in time to see Miriam's locker door swing wide.

Hanging from a magnetic hook, Mag spied a set of car keys, fixed the locker number firmly in her mind, and waited for her chance.

With Lydia trailing behind, Miriam finally hit the showers, leaving Mag to make a choice. Penelope Starr was not the boss of her, and if she pushed the issue, Mag had no problem pushing back. But this was her town now, and she surprised herself with how much she wanted to fit in with the good people of Harmony.

Mag Balefire, social butterfly. Okay, probably not. But maybe she could handle being a social caterpillar. Maybe.

Not today, though. Today she would continue her rule-breaking streak because her chance to do otherwise never came. The bright voices of Miriam and Lydia floated down the short hallway, bounced off the walls, and proved there was only time for magic.

Gathering power from the heat of her blood and the ball of fire in her belly, Mag sent a spear of intention toward the locker.

The solid weight of the keys slid into her hand just as Clara caught up and Mrs. May rounded the corner dressed in a hot pink towel the size of a bed sheet.

"Come on," Mag dragged Clara toward the toilets and into the largest stall, cast a glamour to hide their feet, and whispered, "Fine lot of help you are. Leaving me to do all the work. I snagged these."

Flattened palm up, Mag displayed Miriam's keys. "Shiny, no?"

The rhinestone-encrusted fob was the size of a golf ball, and if the glitter of fake jewels wasn't enough to catch the eye, the brightly patterned keys put it over the top. Mag wondered where a person could buy a tie-dyed house key in the shape of a peace sign. She wanted one of those for herself.

"Miriam's not going anywhere without these. Now what do we do?"

Waving her hand to get back into street clothes, Clara said, "We wait and see."

Ten minutes stuffed into a bathroom stall together hadn't been on Clara's agenda for the day. She loved her sister, but there was such a thing as too much closeness.

"I swear you have the boniest elbows on the planet," Clara nudged Mag's arm away.

"Well, you're breathing in my ear. What did you have for breakfast, anyway? Onions on garlic? Ever heard of mouthwash? Or a toothbrush?"

A furious shoving match ended with Mag's eye pressed to the crack in the door while Clara sat on the toilet lid and waited for the all-clear.

"It's just Lydia and Miriam tearing apart her locker. Let's go."

Clara needed no further urging and vacated the cramped space happily.

"Is something wrong?" Her cheerful smile was met with the panicked look of one who has a chronic problem misplacing things.

"I've lost my keys." Miriam fisted her hands on her hips and surveyed the area around her locker.

"Again," Lydia supplied helpfully.

"What do they look like? We're happy to help you hunt for them." Sweet and innocent, Mag made the offer and suppressed a smile at Miriam's toned-down description of her keys.

"I don't know what's come over me lately. It's been one catastrophe after another. Can you believe I ran my glasses through the laundry? Twice. Wash *and* dry." Miriam shook her head and dumped the contents of her gym bag out on the bench to sort through with frustrated motions.

When the keys didn't turn up, she whirled and slumped down on top of the messy pile. "We're thinking of moving. The town of Harmony doesn't feel like a safe place anymore. Two murders in a row? How does that happen in a place like this?"

Miriam saved Mag or Clara the trouble of trying to shoehorn their choice of topic into the conversation.

"Did you know him well? Taylor Dean, I mean." Going through the motions of continuing the search, Clara angled her body so she could see the look on Miriam's face when she answered.

"What? No. I mean, in a town the size of this you know just about everyone well enough to talk about the weather, but he wasn't what you'd call a friend."

If not for the sheaf of photographs proving there was more to it than Miriam let on, Mag might have missed the hint of bitterness running through her tone. Hiding an affair with her best friend's husband must have increased Miriam's skills in guarding her emotions.

What Mag didn't miss was the look that passed between Lydia and Miriam, and she made a snap decision.

"Found them." Faking the find, she dangled the gaudy keys in front of Miriam's face. Must have slipped into that front pocket and you missed them." She ignored Mrs. May's puzzled frown and the fact that she'd watched the woman search those pockets at least twice. "Clarie, we're going to be late. Shall we?"

Mag dragged Clara around the corner, pulled out the pop-tab silencing charm she always carried and waited for her sister to do the same. A squeeze activated the charm, and then Mag said, "Wait and listen. My instincts are chattering."

Sure enough, the second they thought they were alone, Miriam and Lydia engaged in a whispered conversation.

"Why did you have to bring him into the conversation? With Taylor dead, all our troubles are over," Lydia hissed.

"I know, but he didn't just keel over from natural causes. Someone killed him. Don't you know what that means? If anyone found out he'd tried to blackmail me, the cops would haul me in for questioning, and we'd all be in the hot seat." Even at a whisper, Miriam's voice was shrill.

"Well, you didn't pay the blackmail, and you didn't kill the man, for Pete's sake, and we all have iron-clad alibis for the time of the murder," Lydia said. "Greg isn't a suspect. Can't swing a golf club with a broken wrist. Leonard was at work, and our golf instructor already told the cops we were on the driving range the whole time."

"I know that, but I'd rather the entire town didn't learn about our extracurricular activities. Do you think he tried to blackmail someone else and they didn't want to pay? I mean, if you'd seen the look on his face when I told him I had nothing to hide from my husband and what four consenting adults choose to do in the confines of their own homes wasn't any of his business … he went from smug to pissed off pretty fast."

Lydia shrugged, "I think Leonard put him in his place. Told him he could go right ahead and talk, but if he did, Chief Cobb would find out he'd been stealing packages from the mail truck. That was the end of it."

Aha, Mag thought, *if Leonard knew about the thefts, maybe there were others. Maybe the killer knew.*

There was a short pause before Miriam replied. "I feel bad I didn't go to the police anyway. It might have helped them find someone else with a motive for murder. He wasn't a good person, but does that really mean he deserved to die?"

Whatever Lydia's answer might have been, Mag and Clara didn't get to learn because another group of bathers passed them on their way into the locker room.

"Well, that was a bust." Mag declared when they were safely outside. She sounded a little disappointed. "Other than learning a juicy piece of gossip, anyway. Swingers. Right in the town of Harmony."

Clara cringed at the visual. "And I'm not sure I'll ever look at Leonard Wayland the same way again. But I disagree about it being a bust. We just ruled out four people, right? They all had alibis, right?"

Mag snorted, "Yeah, but that means we're no closer to finding the real killer. And there's still one thing bothering me. That confrontation between Taylor and Leonard. He's a teacher, so what if Taylor threatened to expose their 'extracurricular activities' to the entire town?"

Now that the coast was clear, the sisters exited the locker room while Mag considered what they'd learned. "It would be a scandal. Possibly a major one, but I can't see any way around him being in the classroom at the time of the murder."

"Personally, I think we'd be better off moving on to Reggie Blackthorne. Do we have any proof of where he went after Taylor called the postmaster to report the damage to the truck?" Playing back over everything they already knew, Clara didn't think so.

"No, and I think it bears looking into to see why the cops ruled him out."

Chapter Twelve

Working their way from the spa around to the tennis courts and back to the main office, the sisters could see that Rolling Hills took great care to make their members comfortable while keeping the staff-to-guest ratio at the perfect median level.

Had they required assistance, there were enough welcoming, khaki-shorted and white polo-clad employees on site to accommodate almost immediately, yet Mag and Clara weren't inundated with greetings to a point of irritation—a delicate balance many businesses couldn't seem to find.

Mag was just about to insist on returning to the bus when she heard the trill of the kind of laugh that comes when someone has just said something mean or scandalous. Turning, she spotted three of the youngest coven members lunching on a dining room-adjacent outside patio. Faces carefully turned and eyes that looked anywhere but at her meant she or Clara had been the butt of the joke.

"We really should say hello. Double Bubble just spotted us, and it will seem rude if we don't."

Clara's mouth quirked into a disbelieving grin, "Who now?"

"Double Bubble. The one who's always chewing away on a wad of gum."

"She has a name."

"What is it, then?"

"Wisteria? Mysteria? Oh hell, something like that." Her bluff called, Clara's face went slightly pink.

"Listeria?" Sounded familiar to Mag.

"Now you've resorted to rhymes. And Listeria's a bacteria, not a name."

The hastily whispered conversation continued while their steps took them closer to the patio.

"It's a name for a bacteria, isn't it? I guess Double Bubble is close enough and that one is Toil, and over there is Trouble. Look how they go. Toil is constantly picking at things. See how she straightens out the utensils? Trouble is the one with the sour look. Together they're sublime if you think about it."

"Toil is Winifred Owens, and the pretty one is Selena Sanderson. You're going to have to take the time to learn more about the coven if you're going to be an effective member."

Mag bristled at the gentle scolding.

"When they do something worthy of my notice, I'll remember their names." That last Mag hissed just before she and Clara came within earshot of the cluster of younger women. "For now though, we have to be polite, don't we?"

"If you want to use that excuse, be my guest, but I'd eat my own shoe if I thought you actually gave a damn about Miss Manners's rules of social etiquette."

"Can it, Clarie!" Mag looked down at her ensemble, knew it wouldn't match up the crisp, pastel-trimmed tennis whites sported by the lunching ladies, and wondered if she cared what they thought.

"Good morning, ladies." With apparent difficulty, Mag leaned on her cane to navigate the two short steps up onto the patio and deposited herself with a sigh onto one of the metal chairs at the next table from the young witches. Clara followed suit and flashed a sunny smile.

"Is it true the mailman died right over there?" Double Bubble nodded in the general direction of the scene of the crime and laid down her fork to listen eagerly for any hint of scandal. "And you're the ones who found the body?"

The question she really wanted to ask, Mag thought as she observed the younger woman's eyes searching Clara's face, had more to do with the history of how her sister managed to get de-stoned.

A cardinal sin, the killing of one witch by another came with immediate and irrevocable punishment—the murdering witch was turned to stone. Never had a stoned witch returned to take her place among the living until Clara Balefire had been proven innocent.

As it turned out, her stoning had been of the faux variety, and the unhappy result of magical mishap during a knock-down drag-out fight with her daughter. Intention combined with split-second bad timing, and both mother and daughter had paid the price.

For Clara, that meant spending twenty-five years as living rock while Sylvana was imprisoned in a portal. While neither witch would have declared innocence, neither had committed a mortal sin, either.

Since Clara preferred to let people think what they liked, she ignored the way certain eyes never met hers, but it burned Mag's butt every single time.

"It's true," Mag confirmed tersely.

Pressed for details, the Balefires gave a watered down version of the story.

"I know everyone has a bad mail story, but he helped me once." Selena Sanderson sighed. If Mag had to come up for a name for her, it would have been Blondie McPerky. Right on the cusp of her twenty-fifth birthday, the young witch would spend the next thirty years looking like she should be walking a runway. Not that Mag envied her or anything.

Her sour look had turned nostalgic. "I was eleven or twelve at the time and riding my bike out toward the old mill when I hit a patch of loose gravel and wiped out. I'd bent one of the rims, scraped my leg up something fierce, and sprained my wrist.

When Mr. Dean came along, I was limping home and trying not to cry. He saw me and stopped to help. Put my bike up on the roof of the mail truck, and moved things so I had a place to sit, and he turned right around and took me home. All the rumors can't be true if he'd do a thing like that."

Selena had a lot to learn about the ways of the world, but that she believed the best about a man most had been willing to vilify made Clara think more highly of her. Didn't change her opinion of Taylor Dean much, though. He'd stolen from Mag, and by the looks of the back of his mail truck the day he died, had been checking packages for more things to steal.

Not that she thought he deserved a brutal death for his sins, or that his poor wife should be thrust into such drama. For Babette's sake, the Balefires were on the case, but Clara also felt as if finding his killer would go some way toward paying penance for uncharitable thoughts toward the man. Everyone has some good in them, she supposed, even thieves and blackmailers.

"My hip is acting up again, Clara. Let's go." Abruptly, Mag used what had come to be known as a code phrase to escape sticky situations, but this time Clara recognized it for what it was—more than just an easy getaway from a conversation. Mag's gaze had caught on something in the background.

They bade the women goodbye, and Mag made a beeline for the opposite direction of the parking lot.

"What's going on?" Clara asked, huffing and puffing after her sister.

"Honey-pixie sighting," she said, jabbing her chin to an area somewhere ahead and to the right. "A pair of mates, and we're lucky none of those women recognized them for what they are. It's pretty clear none of those girls possesses the wherewithal to have killed Taylor, so there's nothing more to be discovered listening to them prattle on. And, we don't need Penelope shoved any further up our badonkadonks than absolutely necessary."

"You know Hagatha's anti-cussing charm doesn't reach this far, right?"

"I've come around on that particular term, and now I find it sort of amusing if it's all the same to you."

Clara lifted her hands in mock surrender. "No skin off my nose if you want to sound like a thirteen-year-old boy." She followed Mag, who had waited until they were under deep tree cover to conjure a large butterfly net and a gilt-trimmed cage thrumming with magic.

"Need some bait." Mag dug through her magically deep pockets and began pulling out jars, potion bottles, and packets.

"No wonder you walk like you're dragging the weight of the world," Clara observed as the pile grew larger. "You're carrying half a workshop's worth of ingredients in there. What is all that stuff?"

"A few odds and ends. Things too dangerous to leave unprotected."

"Oh, Maggie," she said, her heart going out to her sister, "I feel like you've been too much alone. When we get home, we're going to make a charmed safe for your stockpile. Get some of the weight off that leg and give it a better chance to heal. You should have told me you needed more space in the workroom."

"Old habits run deep." Mag's tone was gruff as she continued to dig through her pockets.

"Now, what are we looking for?" Clara picked up an amber jar and peered inside, then jumped back slightly when a blinking eye peered back.

"Andruvian trumpet flower." A hint of a smirk played over Mag's lips.

"Where did you find one of those?" Considering they only grew on the southeastern slope of the Andruvian mountains deep in the heart of the Faelands and were protected besides, Mag having one smacked of scandal.

"I didn't find it. It was a gift." And the great Margaret Balefire blushed.

Clara's eyes widened. "From a man?" Mag's blush deepened, and Clara learned something new about her sister. Somewhere under all the bluff and bluster lay a sentimental streak if she was carrying around a flower given to her by a beau.

"Get the stars out of your eyes and help me find it. Never met a pixie could turn down a taste of Andruvian nectar."

For now, Clara let it slide, but there was a story, and she planned to dig it out of her sister eventually. It took a few minutes of sorting, but Mag finally turned up the crystal potion bottle containing the perfectly-preserved flower.

"Got it." A wave of her hand cleared the jumble of items.

Delicate petals of palest porcelain pink freckled with wine-red spots curved into a trumpet-shaped cup that contained a pool of nectar that smelled of everything sweet. Holding the flower up to the sun revealed a miniature rainbow arching across the top of the belled opening. It was a lovely thing, and Clara sighed at the sight.

"Now we need to find just the right spot."

They spent another few minutes finding a clearing where the sun slanted through the trees and creating a mound of fern fronds in which to nestle the bait, then Clara conjured a fan. A few waves of the pleated paper directed the enticing scent of the nectar in the direction she'd last seen the pixies hovering. She pulled the old pop tab out of her pocket for the second time that day, rubbed it to activate the charm that silenced her footsteps, and waited for Clara do to the same.

"And now we wait."

Not for long. With a buzzing of wings and the twitter of tiny voices, the pair of pixies zipped into the clearing and arrowed toward their doom. Okay, maybe not doom, since the Balefires meant them no actual harm, but capture, for sure.

Clara, armed with the net while Mag had taken control of the cage, crept closer and tried to stay out of the pixies line of sight. She needn't have bothered, though, since the liquid carried intoxicating properties and by the time she was close enough to deploy the net, both pixies lay draped over each other, fast asleep.

Into the cage they went while Mag carefully re-bottled the flower, and when she ran a finger over the petals with the faintest look of regret on her face, Clara declined to comment. She picked up the cage, slung an arm around her sister, and took them home.

Chapter Thirteen

Despite her insistence that participation in several community organizations and clubs hadn't begun to take over her life when it came time for the next crocheting club meeting, Clara had to admit her schedule had become tight enough to force a game of Sophie's choice.

Inconveniently, both Pyewacket and Jinx had skedaddled off somewhere, so asking them to spend the day tending the backyard garden wasn't an option. Not that it mattered.

If history repeated, they'd get one-tenth of the way through the project and end up chasing butterflies anyway. *If you want something done right, it's best to do it yourself,* she thought.

Clara sighed, loathe to approach her sister with the type of request she was about to make. "Maggie, I could use your superior problem-solving skills, if you don't mind." A little flattery always proved indispensable.

Or maybe not.

Mag smirked at her. "What exactly do you want, Clara? Your nose has a brown stain on it, and I'm not stupid enough to believe you can't decide on your own."

"Fine," Clara retorted, "I need you to go to crocheting club today. By yourself."

"Why on earth would I agree to that?" Mag's eyebrows arched then beetled into a frown.

"Because Babette Dean is a member, and I think it's our best shot of learning anything useful about the case."

"You can't do that yourself? I was planning to tail Reggie Blackthorne today."

"I have weeding to do. Work that nets us an income, and more importantly gives me the ingredients I need for your hip cream. If I let it go any longer, the stinging nettle crop will be ruined.

Clara heaved a sigh. "The best growing conditions are in that corner spot along the back fence, so it has to be done the old-fashioned way. No magic in public, remember? Mrs. Green has been camped in front of her telescope all week. It's a good thing her eyesight isn't what it used to be, or she'd be telling everyone in town there's something funny about those Balefire cats."

With a wicked twinkle in her eye, Clara added, "Or you could weed the nettles for me and I'll go instead." Mag's distaste for the prickly plants ran deep and would either outweigh her reluctance for social interaction or not. Clara was betting it would.

"What are we hoping to learn, and what makes you think Babette would unburden her soul to me?"

"You've spent a good portion of your life persuading people to do things they don't want to do. I think you'll figure out a way to see if she has any fresh ideas about the killer. Besides, she likes you since you gave her all that money for the writing box."

"Don't remind me, Clarie." Mag considered Clara's request, and in an uncharacteristic display of remorse for all of the griping she'd put her sister through, agreed to attend the meeting.

At least that's the way she played it. Clara knew better.

She also knew her sister thought Babette would be the best source of information on whether Chief Cobb had moved on in the investigation. If he didn't back off, Mag swore she would turn him into a toad and dump him in the swamp behind the post office.

That was how it happened that Mag was alone as she trudged along Mystic Street leaning heavily on her cane.

She made quite a picture with a knitting bag slung across her chest, her free hand waving a battery-operated, personal misting fan she'd picked up at the drugstore one intolerably hot afternoon. Anyone driving by might have thought her an escapee from an assisted living facility, in her floppy sun hat and orthopedic shoes.

The inside of the Harmony town library smelled too clean and not of musty paper as such establishments had in Mag's day. She silently cursed the digital age for being well on the way to rendering parchment and wax obsolete.

What would be the fate of the library without books?

"Welcome back." Seated alone in the room, Maude Prescott didn't seem surprised that, after her show of rebellion at the last meeting, Mag had returned for a second go-round. "Needles or hooks today, Margaret?" She asked with a straight face.

Mag's curiosity was piqued. There was something disconcerting about Maude's demeanor. It was rare that a regular human could catch her off-guard, but for all the world, Mag couldn't tell when the woman was being serious or sarcastic.

"I'll be knitting if nobody objects." But she'd wield the needles with a bit less disruptive force this time around.

Maude gave a sharp, approving nod. "A woman after my own heart, sticking to your guns. Screw 'em all, I always say. I do as I please, and if someone doesn't like it, well that's just too darned bad."

Just as Mag was cracking a smile and thinking she might have finally met a kindred spirit in the straight-laced town of Harmony, Babette Dean ducked inside the meeting room.

Maude glanced in the direction of the door, "Poor thing," She murmured, shaking her head sadly.

"Yes, poor thing indeed," Mag mused, "Though perhaps she's better off now." The words fell from her lips before common sense kicked in. Maybe Clara was right, and she really did suffer from a bad case of verbal incontinence. "I didn't mean that the way it sounded."

"Don't mince words on my account. Taylor Dean wasn't exactly a pillar of the community. Do you know how many months in a row he didn't deliver my fruit-of-the-month basket? It's not as though Tosca pears grow on trees. At least not in New England. Untrustworthy, he was. Dollars to donuts he had some skeletons in his closet. Babette will be just fine now."

Mag nodded in agreement. "Time heals many wounds." She knew better than most that it couldn't heal them all, but hoped that wouldn't be the case for Babette.

As the rest of the group filed in, Mag took a seat and motioned for Babette to join her, and was surprised when the widow appeared relieved and plopped down in the proffered chair. Now flanked by two new potential friends, Mag was starting to understand why Clara was so willing to participate in town clubs.

"Thanks," Babette said, releasing a big breath. "You have no idea how nice it is to see a friendly face. Everywhere I go these days, people stop talking and stare with either malice or pity. It's exhausting."

"People still think you're responsible for your husband's death? I thought you'd been cleared by the police." Mag's hackles went up, and some uncharitable thoughts about Chief Cobb flitted through her mind.

Babette nodded, "Officially, yes, but that won't stop the rumor mill, and now the police are getting annoyed with me because I don't have any helpful information. They keep asking for a name, but I can't imagine who would want to hurt my Taylor."

Babette answered Mag's next question before she had a chance to ask if there were any new suspects. The widow's eyes carried a perpetual rim of red these days and it took very little for them to well up with a fresh barrage of tears.

A short silence fell while Babette pulled herself together.

After a few sniffs, she said to Mag, "How did you know I'd been cleared? Chief Cobb only made it official today."

This is what you get when you make friends, Mag thought. *A case of the loose lips.*

"He showed up at my place asking questions. Grasping at straws, he was, since last I knew, it wasn't a crime to tell someone they were bad at their job. No offense intended." Mag lowered the heat when she heard a snort from Maude. Social niceties. Bah.

When the widow relinquished her seat for a cup of sludge labeled coffee, Maude whispered to Mag, "You shouldn't feel bad for speaking your mind. If telling Taylor Dean he was a lousy mailman was a crime, half the town will be on trial. This murder might never be solved."

"Well, *someone* bashed the poor lout over the head. Whoever it was must have left a clue. Nobody is that careful."

Maude nodded in agreement but dropped the subject when Babette returned to apply hook to yarn.

It was at about that time Mag realized most of the crocheters were working off the same pattern and turning out a series of small, rounded sacks with drawstring closures at as furious a pace as they could manage.

"What are you all making?" Asking in spite of herself, Mag wasn't sure she wanted to know.

"Club cozies," Babette's reply was the most cheerful Mag had ever heard her sound. And provided no useful information whatsoever.

When Mag's response only included repeating the term in a questioning voice, Gertrude Granger elaborated.

"Golf club cozies. We run an annual sale at the club's pro shop, and the proceeds all go to charity. We're getting geared up for this year's sale."

Naturally, Gertrude's contributions looked like candy canes.

"And people actually pay money for them?" She hadn't meant it to come out as an insult, but Mag knew it sounded that way the second the question left her lips. "They're lovely, but what do they do?"

"Protect the clubs during transport," Maude answered, and Mag nodded.

Conversation turned to civic matters, and it was amid the clicking of Mag's knitting needles and the silent working of a dozen crochet hooks that she realized how things really got done in the small town of Harmony.

Within a half hour, the group had verbally drafted a petition to force Reggie Blackthorne into filling in the pothole at the end of Victory Lane.

The conversation flowed around Mag, who hadn't bothered to put names to all the faces and had too little experience with Harmony's inner workings to provide any input.

Still, she listened closely in case there was a chance to glean any useful information.

How that man gets away with such substandard work is a mystery to me.

Toss in a handful of loose patch and not even bother to tamp it down. Disgraceful.

Should give more business to that young fellow over in Blanville. My sister says he's doing a great job on the roads.

Talk to the planning committee, but you'll be wasting your breath. They won't give the work to anyone else.

When Mag left the library an hour later, she had more questions than answers about why Reggie Blackthorne's name had been in Taylor Dean's book, and she was also carrying a golf-cozy pattern.

Clara might not be happy about it, but Mag had volunteered her to make two dozen of them before the next meeting. Without remorse.

Chapter Fourteen

Back at Balms and Bygones, the sisters closed the shop half an hour early when a sudden, drenching downpour effectively killed business for the day.

Taking advantage of the extra time, they set about getting things restocked and ready for the next morning. While they worked, they mulled over all the evidence collected so far, and concluded it was time to look more deeply into Reggie Blackthorne.

A ruckus coming from the back room alerting Mag and Clara to Hagatha's presence, interrupting the debate on how to do that without raising suspicion.

Well, the ruckus and the buzz of a honey pixie's wings beating outside the window. A big one if it made that much noise even through glass.

Over the past few weeks, the sister witches had stopped expecting to find a dangerous intruder of the garden variety and still couldn't figure out a way to keep Hagatha from trespassing. It must have been or Hagatha to give up the home she'd had since before Harmony became a town and move in with her niece.

It was clear Romilda Crow possessed a less than watchful eye, considering Hagatha continued to break back into her old house at least three times a week. Mag wondered whether she would have the nerve to behave that way had the place been purchased by a non-witch, and had come to the conclusion that Hagatha would never have allowed that to happen in the first place.

"Hagatha, what are you doing here? You know you're supposed to warn us before you pop over." Clara called hesitantly. "If she's messing with my product supply again, I swear to the Goddess you're going to have to hold me back from ripping her head off." She muttered under her breath to Mag.

"I heard that, little Missy. Any day you think you can take me, I'm happy to rise to the challenge." Hagatha poked her head out of the supply room and directed a pointed look at Clara, whose confidence wavered under the intense heat.

She knew good and well Hagatha's power was far greater than her own, and possibly hers and Mag's combined. If that were the case, attempts to sabotage her exploits were likely to prove futile.

Unless Hagatha wanted them sabotaged, and Clara wouldn't put it past the old crone to have motives layered under motives.

"I just needed to borrow a little bit of combustion powder. Romilda won't let me keep it in the house. Thinks I'm going to burn the place down or something."

Mag and Clara exchanged a worried look. "What exactly do you need it for?"

"Why, the honey pixies, of course." Hagatha had a way of making both the Balefire sisters feel like children, even though half of what came out of her mouth sounded like complete nonsense. Well, at first anyway.

The rest evoked an uncomfortable feeling of dread.

"This particular breed lives in the section of the Faelands where fire and water meet. During the mild months of what's considered winter there, they pollinate a jungle-like area surrounded by beaches. In the summer, they migrate south and copulate amid exploding geysers of lava. The males who don't get burned to a crisp are considered the cream of the crop and can have their pick of the females. I thought you said you were familiar with this species, Margaret."

Chagrined, Mag scowled in Hagatha's direction but declined to respond. Instead, she passed her sister the proverbial baton, an unspoken *Tag, you're it* evident in her expression. While Clara attempted to talk Hagatha into displaying a modicum of caution, Mag began to tidy up the shop for the next day's business.

Clara's turn with Hagatha lasted under five minutes before she claimed to hear Pye calling and escaped the room without looking back.

"Mag, you know where we keep the supplies, if you could just … I'll be right back."

And if Mag believed that, she was three kinds of a fool.

Turning to Hagatha, she said, "How much do you need?"

"Half an ounce should do it." There's a look a kid gets when asking for cake before dinner—half hopeful and half pure mischief—and Hagatha's face sporting that expression creeped Mag out more than a little.

"That's enough to blow up the whole town. Try again."

"Fine. Ten grains, then. Okay? What a killjoy." A potion bottle appeared in Hagatha's hand and she lifted an eyebrow when Mag opened it and took a sniff to make sure it was clean. "You know, not a lot of witches would have known to check for aconite or sulfur residue."

"Not my first time," was all Mag would admit. "Listen, you've been in this town practically forever. What can you tell me about Reggie Blackthorne?"

Even after a late-night brainstorming session, the Balefires hadn't come up with a way to verify Reggie's whereabouts at the time of the murder.

"He had chubby thighs when he was a baby." A prompt and useless reply.

Mag closed her eyes, took a deep breath, and asked the goddess for patience before elaborating. "I could have done without that mental image."

The problem with old Reggie was that Mag couldn't see him for the murder. Nothing about him was ringing her bad-guy bell, and there was no one other than Hagatha she knew well enough to pump for information.

She tried a different tack. "Who do you like for the mailman's murder?"

"Not Reggie Blackthorne, if that's what you're asking. He's crafty, but not mean enough for murder." Hagatha confirmed Mag's impressions.

"Even if Taylor Dean were in possession of sensitive information, Reggie wouldn't want made public? Everyone has their breaking point."

"Blackmail is it?" Conjuring up an old cotton pillowcase in a pretty rose pattern, Hagatha used it to cushion the vial of combustion powder. The resulting ball of cloth disappeared into her pocket.

"It's a theory." Mag wondered if she should have held out for only five grains of the volatile substance, but it was too late for that now. "But I have no evidence."

Wanting to take the conversation out of Clara's earshot, Mag gestured for Hagatha to follow her out the back door.

A slanting ray of sunlight filtered through the slate blue of dispersing rain clouds, lighting the gardens up as if they were covered in diamond dust.

Out of the line of Mrs. Green's sight, Mag flicked her wrist as if tossing a yo-yo made out of Balefire. Flickering tongues of heat licked over a pair of cast iron patio chairs and dried them thoroughly enough for both witches to take a seat.

"What are you waiting for? Christmas?"

"I'm walking a line here." Hoping she wouldn't end up being cursed into the middle of next week, Mag faced off against Hagatha. "You don't have to tell me what you'd do in this circumstance because I already know.

Slap him with a truth spell, or a compulsion charm, and he'd fall all over himself to confess his every sin."

"Bet your booty."

Mag stifled a chuckle over Hagatha's command of outdated slang, and let some of the tension fall out of her shoulders. "And if he's not the murderer? Where would that fall on the scale of harming none?"

Hagatha's answer, as illuminating as it might have been, never came, because a honey pixie dropped out of the sky to land on her shoulder. It cast a baleful eye at Mag, fluttered wings that glistened with an inner light, and grasped the curl of Hagatha's ear with a tiny hand.

Leaning close, the pixie spoke in a fluting voice and whatever it said put a wide grin on Hagatha's face.

Another spate fell into Hagatha's ear while the pixie continued to look at Mag, this time ending on an upward note that sounded like a question and her little face softened with hope.

"Maypole wonders if she might be allowed access to a small corner of your dill bed." Hagatha translated. "She says you have some of the fernleaf variety."

Mag raised an eyebrow, "Dill weed?"

"Not a weed and not just for pickles. The flowers carry small amounts of pollen. It's considered a delicacy, and the fernleaf type is an essential ingredient in producing the healing serum that goes into their honey." A first for Mag, seeing Hagatha go into teaching mode. The old girl must have been something in her day.

"With the right combination of pollen and nectar, pixie honey has amazing curative properties—wound healing, counteracts certain poisons. It's said a pixie-honey potion could bring a person back from the brink of death."

Hagatha gave Mag a saucy wink, "Puts the wood back in a man's stem, too. Gives him plenty of staying power, if you know what I mean." Mag wished she didn't.

"The mature females like to crush dill fronds and rub the oils on their skin on for the scent. Draws the males like flies to a fresh pile."

"Tell her to knock herself out." Mag waved a hand to indicate the direction and watched the tiny body flit in a zigzag down the path. Soon her nose picked up the sharp and tangy scent of dill wafting on the breeze.

"What was that all about? And don't tell me the only reason she showed up here had to do with raiding my gardens for medicinal herbs."

Mag had to ask because she'd bet her last dollar the pixie farming had nothing to do with keeping down the mosquito population.

"I'll be honest, I brought them here for the pest control, but they've proved useful in other areas. They're small, and they can be quiet when they want to be. There's one sitting on the edge of the rain gutter not three feet over your head, and you never noticed." Hagatha pointed upwards.

"Spies. You've cultivated an army of spies." Immediate tension corded Mag's shoulder muscles, and she felt a headache inching up toward the back of her eyes. "Great goddess, Haggie. That's—"

And then she thought about it.

"Genius."

"If I do say so myself," Hagatha agreed. "It's a good thing you released the pair you caught, too. And don't worry, your secrets are safe with me."

Hades' teeth, what had she said in front of the big-mouthed denizens of Fae? A frantic search of her memory turned up nothing more damning than her opinion of Hagatha's mental faculties. Nothing, she was certain, the old witch hadn't heard from multiple sources.

"Then you'll get them to help me?" Mag implored.

Hagatha didn't miss a beat, "What's in it for me?"

Feeling her butt settle into that unenviable spot between the rock and the hard place, Mag offered the tentative answer, "it would be fun." She waited for Haggie to decide.

"Throw in another ten, and we have a deal."

Feeling like she'd struck a bargain with a crossroads demon, Mag added ten more grains of combustion powder to the vial. If the town of Harmony got blown off the map, at least she'd go with it and not have to face an angry mob later.

Cold consolation.

"How do you get them to do the work? It can't all be about bribing them with dill." Mag sailed right past the point of no return and threw her lot in with Hagatha.

It wouldn't be mosquitoes biting her in the butt if this went south, but what was life without a little risk? Boring. That's what.

"Best you leave that to me, and I'll handle the payment." What went unspoken—yet fully understood—was that Mag would be better off not knowing certain details of the arrangement. "Get me within fifty feet of him, and we're in business."

That was how it came to be that with Mag behind the wheel and Hagatha riding shotgun, leaving Clara none the wiser, the VW bus rolled out from behind Balms and Bygones on a mission.

"Any idea where we're going?" Hanging on for dear life, Hagatha's voice quavered a little.

"As it happens, I know where the crew should be today, and I'm betting the rain delayed them enough this afternoon that they'll still be there trying to hit a deadline. Rolling Hills Road. It's our best bet."

Applying the gas pedal with abandon, Mag sent the bus rocketing toward the golf course, and coincidentally, toward the scene of Taylor's murder. Funny how things come full circle sometimes.

There was Reggie's truck in all its overblown glory, parked along the side of the road. The man himself strutted around with a shovel in his hand but never seemed to apply the tool to any use.

"There he is. Now what? Can you deploy the pixies from here?" Deploy the pixies. A combination of words Mag never expected to say.

"Drive on past and pull into the turnaround down by the cement bridge where I can have a little privacy."

Before the bus came to a final halt, Hagatha let out a whistle that raised the hairs on the back of Mag's neck and set her back teeth vibrating.

"A little warning might have been nice," she said once the sound died away.

"Duck," was Hagatha's reply and delivered with a sardonically raised brow.

"Huh?" A second too late, Mag caught on. The first of six pixies managed to pull up but the second got tangled up in the fuzzy white strands of her hair. "Ow! That hurts."

A minute or two passed painfully while Mag and the pixie worked to untangle from each other and Hagatha shook with silent mirth.

"It's not funny," Mag groused, touching her scalp to make sure she didn't have a bald spot.

"Told you to duck." Not much to argue with there, so Mag let it go. "Get out and come around to my side," Hagatha said. "Hold your arms out, and once they land on you, don't make any sudden moves."

A thrill of anticipation tickled over Mag's skin. Apprentice pixie whisperer, that's what she was about to become. She did as she was told and listened to the series of hoots and whistles that she assumed was Hagatha speaking their language.

Finally, at a nod from the wizened witch, a flutter of iridescent bodies touched down upon her arms, their tiny toes pinching as they dug in for purchase, but Mag never flinched. She stood next to the bus window and waited for instructions.

"Now what?" Fae energy tingled along the tips of Mag's ears and fingertips.

"Take them just far enough so you can see Reggie, but stay out of sight. Here, this should help." Without warning, Hagatha spit into Mag's left eye. As Mag blinked to clear away the gob of saliva, her vision sharpened measurably.

"Nice trick. You'll have to teach me that one."

"Nothing to it. Two parts pine pitch to one part powdered yak hair, with a splash of carrot juice. I keep a wad between my cheek and gums for just such occasions. Once you have him in your sights, give them the all-clear, and they'll go scout around and report back anything they hear. Piece of cake."

Sounded easy enough, so Mag—minus the ever-present cane and moving slowly for its loss—made her way back toward the construction crew and her quarry. She only bobbled once, and got a vicious pinch for her efforts before the figure of Reggie Blackthorne appeared in the distance.

Mag halted and made ready to give the pixies the signal when she realized Hagatha had neglected to tell her what it was. Frozen with her arms outstretched and feeling the pressure in her shoulders to hold them in position, she cursed the old witch and decided to try a few things before making a pixie-laden return trip.

"Hsst!" didn't work. Neither did any other voice command she tried. Finally, arms aching with effort, she gave them a little flap to demonstrate the pixies should do the same. Off they flew, leaving a few welts to mar her skin.

"Old bat. I swear that women is demon-born." Mag returned to the VW and shot Hagatha a dirty look while she rubbed at the painful spots.

"What are we sitting here for?" Hagatha's voice cracked the silence. "Maypole will find me when she's ready. Take me back to your place."

Passing back through the construction zone, Mag waggled her fingers and grinned at Reggie who paid no attention to the birdlike creatures flitting over his head. If she'd had any forethought, she'd have tried harder to make friends with the pixies instead of caging a couple of them for a short while. Handy creatures to have around if you didn't turn them into enemies.

Maypole beat them home by a matter of minutes, according to Clara, who had no idea why the pixie had been trying to get into the house the whole time.

"It's like we're under siege," she complained. "Hagatha, call off your minion if you please."

"At the moment, she's our minion." There wasn't time to explain, so Mag popped the screen and watched Maypole settle on Hagatha's shoulder to preen her feathers and chitter away.

"Well?" Mag asked, tired of waiting. "What did she learn? She can have all the dill she wants."

Clara looked back and forth between Mag and Hagatha with dismay written all over her face. As far as she was concerned, Hagatha had lured her sister over to the dark side.

No one was more surprised when Maypole opened her mouth, and Reggie Blackthorne's voice came out. Varying pauses between the sentences indicated multiple phone conversations, but only hearing the parts of them Maypole considered important was enough for the witches to get the gist.

I'll keep them here and get it done. I don't care if they're here until midnight. We had an agreement, and you know for the right price, I always deliver, but I don't control the weather.

No, you're not on the books for tomorrow. It was Rolling Hills first, and if you came through on the rest of the deal, I'd bump the work on your parking lot ahead of Victory Lane. The check cleared and that's enough to put you on the schedule, but I'm not seeing that Prestigio Super7 titanium driver you promised me.

Show me the driver, I'll have the crew there in the morning, and hang the old biddies and their petition. That pothole isn't going anywhere.

Look, I'm not the one who offed the mailman on your property and dragged the cops into your business. For crying out loud, you were with me while the guy was getting offed. Whoever it was did me a favor, but your current predicament isn't my problem.

You want the job started tomorrow, show me a shipping invoice with my name on it first thing in the morning, and I'll have the crew there. Get me the nine instead, and I'll pull in an extra guy, shave a day or two off the job, have it done early.

"Looks like we can cross Reggie off the list," Mag said when Maypole fell silent. "Or turn him for accepting payola."

To the pixies, she said, "Go on, little one, don't destroy anything and you can have the run of the gardens. You and all your friends."

"You're going to have to fill me in how all of this went down," Clara's gaze swiveled between Hagatha and her sister, "but it looks like Reggie is innocent."

Chapter Fifteen

Clara knew trouble was brewing hotter than a size twelve cauldron, even before Chief Cobb and his partner descended upon Balms and Bygones the next morning.

The pricking in her thumbs had started not long after Hagatha, and her pixies went home the night before. Hours spent staring at the unresponsive depths of a crystal ball provided no useful information on the impending threat.

Stubbornly, Clara resisted the urge to go knocking on the door of Mag's hut out back, even if her sister could have predicted the visitor's name, telephone number, and shoe size with only a cursory glance into the smoky sphere.

Divination wasn't one of Clara's strong suits, not that she bemoaned it as a weakness. When it came to the big stuff—for instance, the identity of a murderous psychopath—a quartz crystal would be about as useful as a magic eight ball for even the most gifted witch.

"Speak of the devil, and he shall appear," Mag muttered upon finding Chief Cobb stationed just outside the entrance to the store waiting for someone to unlock the door.

Deputy Nye, who lingered next to her partner, appeared a bit more reserved than she had during her previous encounters with the Balefire sisters, and the fact didn't go unnoticed by either of them.

"When were we speaking of the devil?" Still annoyed with Mag for consorting with Hagatha without bringing her into the loop, Clara hadn't found a lot to say to her sister that morning.

"How can we help you today, officers? Come to throw around more accusations, or do you have a warrant this time?" Mag raised one eyebrow in outright defiance, making Clara wonder whether she was ever going to learn to play nice.

Deputy Nye glanced at Chief Cobb for reassurance, and at his nod took the lead, "May we come inside and ask you a few more questions, please?" Her tone brooked no refusal, so Clara graciously stepped aside to allow them entrance.

This time, however, no offer of refreshment would be forthcoming. Though she disagreed with Mag's method of dealing with the police, she shared her sister's reluctance to cooperate and wished the officers would direct their efforts toward the real murderer.

"Unfortunately, we've been unable to verify your credentials. There is no record of a Margaret or Clara Balefire having been born within the last hundred years, and the Bureau of Motor Vehicles confirmed that neither of you has a valid driver's license. As far as public records go, you two are ghosts." Nye spoke in a matter-of-fact yet gentle tone while a vein in Chief Cobb's forehead throbbed from the effort of staying silent.

Try as he might, Cobb simply couldn't maintain the illusion that his partner held the reigns, "You need to explain yourselves, right now. Just who are you, and how did you manage to acquire this property without valid identification?"

Mag's lip twitched, and it took everything she had not to answer with the truth. Explaining that they had been born in the eighteenth century and had purchased the house from a witch-owned agency who verified identities in a most unorthodox way would only give Cobb the ammunition he needed to have them committed.

"There must have been some clerical error," the lie tripped off Mag's tongue with ease, "Are you sure you spelled Balefire correctly?" She reached into the purse she was still carrying and presented an authentic-looking identification card.

Chief Cobb held it up to the light, looking for a telltale sign of tampering and, finding none, handed the card back to Mag with frustration painted plainly across his face. "This still doesn't explain the lack of paperwork."

"Chief Cobb, with all due respect, my mother is an old-fashioned woman. All of her accounts are still in my father's name." Another total lie stated with ease. "As we said before, come back when you have a warrant or any actual evidence related to this crime."

"Forget about the warrant, if he wants to search the place, let him. He's not going to find anything." Mag challenged, the strength of her tone a direct contradiction to her frail appearance, which did nothing to convince either the chief or deputy of her inability to commit the murder.

Chief Cobb didn't need any further encouragement. In fact, he'd been dying to find out what was inside the house since before Hagatha sold it to the Balefires, which wasn't surprising since the old witch seemed to elicit curiosity by the truckload.

Deputy Nye shot an apologetic smile toward the sisters and began helping Chief Cobb search the parlor first, then move on to Clara's upstairs living quarters.

With the blink of an eye and a flick of her wrist, everything witchy disappeared into thin air. If he wanted to go rooting around in her underwear drawer, all he would find was a few pairs of granny panties and a battery-operated device she'd conjured in an attempt to embarrass him.

Looking as though someone had peed in his Cheerios, and having found nothing of relevance to the crime, the chief moved into the shop to conduct the last part of his search. Checking every nook and cranny, he still came up empty-handed and looked halfway apologetic when he returned to the entrance and removed a pair of disposable gloves from his hands.

Mag turned narrowed eyes on Chief Cobb and was just about to lay into him when something near the door caught his eye. He pulled on a new pair of gloves and yanked a golf club out of the same umbrella rack Babette

Dean had knocked over during her first visit to Balms and Bygones.

"Well, look what we have here. Forensic evidence identified the murder weapon as a golf club just like this one. I think we have enough evidence to take you into custody. Margaret and Clara Balefire—"

A swell of magic lifted Clara's hair, and she instinctively turned to her sister, assuming she had been the one to render Chief Cobb and Deputy Nye frozen in place. To her surprise, Mag looked equally dismayed.

"This is getting more interesting by the day." Hagatha chuckled. "We can't have them dragging you down to the station now, can we?"

"What do you intend to do, turn them into statues as part of the garden decor?" Clara took a tentative step toward the immobile officers. Even the dust motes that had been circling the air around their heads were now suspended in place, as if the time-space continuum surrounding Chief Cobb and Deputy Nye had been displaced.

Hagatha sighed, "Of course not. We need to use a memory charm. It's the only option, don't you agree?"

"It bears consideration," Mag replied.

"Am I the only one who takes the rules seriously?" Clara demanded. "We can't interfere in their free will. As witches, we're expected to harm none. I don't know about you two, but I don't feel like having this come back to me times three."

Intervening for the protection of normals after one of Hagatha's magical mishaps was one thing. Outright casting to protect one's backside was entirely another.

"You young'uns think that every time you cast, the karma police are going to come cart you off to some magical prison. In case it's escaped your attention, the actual police are about to cart you off to actual jail. Now, did either of you whack Taylor Dean with that golf club?" Hagatha retorted.

"Of course not!" Mag exclaimed.

"Didn't think so. But if they've got you in their sights, you're not going to get the chance to find out who the real killer is, and he or she will walk free. There's no reason to resign yourself to that fate if you have the means to stop it." Hagatha said.

"She's got a point, Clarie." Mag looked at her sister with desperation on her face. "Whoever killed Taylor must have found out we're investigating, and obviously wants us stopped. Planting evidence is risky, and that means the murderer is either worried we're getting too close to learning the truth, or they're completely insane. Getting ourselves arrested simply isn't an option."

Mag paused, considering the Chief and his officer, one frozen with a look of self-righteous victory and the other with consternation. "This seems like the lesser of evils. We charm these two to forget about the club, find the killer ourselves, and hand him over on a silver platter. No harm, no foul. No karma."

"I agree we don't have a choice, but you're wrong about the no karma. We're casting on a human for personal gain, even if we find the killer. If you think otherwise, you're kidding yourself. It's going to cost us each one of our own memories and I hope it's worth it."

Everyone has a memory they'd rather lose, but Clara knew the rules of magic carried their own brand of trickery. Spinning this particular wheel could cost her something dear.

"Then I'll do it myself. Half of my memories are lousy anyway." Mag offered to take the bullet.

"No. This is for both of us."

Together Mag and Clara chanted:

On this day and in this hour
We call upon Lethe's might and power
Time turn back their memory
As we will, so mote it be.

Feeding intention into the spell in a steady stream, Clara took the reins and carefully wiped away the period of time that might point Cobb in her or Mag's direction. The process required a delicate touch, making her the best suited for the job.

Remove too little, and you miss the trigger point and set yourself up for the whole problem to loop back around. Remove too much, and you risk causing emotional damage.

When it was done, Clara gently eased the club from Cobb's grasp, whisked it away to a secure spot in her closet, and replaced it with one of Mag's Victorian chamber pots. Just because the visual tickled her sense of humor.

"Okay, I think we're good, Hagatha. Release the spell, but get out of sight before you do. Neither of them will remember you were here, and that can't help but be a good thing."

Grumbling all the way about how some people were nothing more than ungrateful witches who didn't appreciate her, Hagatha stomped through the shop, and out the back. So annoyed was she, she didn't bother to turn around, casting the release of her spell over her shoulder.

Cobb flickered back to life, stared at the chamber pot in his hand, and then at the Balefire sisters with a frown. "What was I saying?"

"I believe you were asking the price of that chamber pot," Mag had trouble biting back a giggle; a situation made worse when Clara shot her a wink. "I'd be happy to give you a discount on it if you like."

"No, I—thank you for your time. I think we'll be leaving now. If you remember anything further, please don't hesitate to call."

Thrusting the ceramic vessel decorated in a distinctly feminine, floral motif into Mag's hands, Chief Cobb left the building with no memory of the umbrella stand or its contents.

When the coast was clear again, Mag twisted the lock on the door but left the open sign facing out so there'd be a clear warning before an errant customer entered the store. Then she turned to Clara. "Well, that was fun." Sarcasm spun out into the room like darts winging toward a bullseye.

Clara conjured the golf club from the closet, and careful not to touch it any more than she already had, settled it on the counter as Hagatha and her walker made a reappearance.

"You didn't have to hide the combustion powder." Ignoring the elephant in the room, she directed her comment to Mag.

"It seems I did. Or you wouldn't know it was missing, now would you?"

"Could we focus on the more immediate problem?" Clara dropped the window shades. For once, she wanted to work magic in peace.

Calling on the source of her power, she sent balefire in a flickering sheen across the surface of the club's handle. If there were any fingerprints to be found, soot from the flame would pick them out.

"Wiped clean by the looks of it," she concluded.

"Or the killer wore gloves." Donning her own pair, the ones she wore when she examined priceless antiques, Mag picked up the club and inspected it more closely.

"If this is even the murder weapon," Hagatha chimed in.

"What would be the point of stashing it here if it wasn't? I think we can safely assume the killer has been in the store."

"Give it here," Hagatha held out a hand. "I just need five minutes and a grain of combustion powder, and I'll tell you everything you need to know."

Mag wasn't fooled.

"Not one grain. Help or don't help, that's up to you."

"Ungrateful witch." Hagatha's assessment of Mag held no heat, presumably because to her, this was high entertainment.

Whispering and muttering to herself, Hagatha tested her mettle against the club's metal with nothing to show for it in the end. Spells of increasing power and complexity failed to reveal even a single piece of evidence save for the presence of blood on the business end.

Well, none that had anything to do with the wielder of the golf club, anyway. She did manage to reveal that Mag wore a girdle under her skirts before she called it quits. Information no one really wanted to know.

Chapter Sixteen

"We'll take it from here, Hagatha." Since the curtains were already closed, Clara suggested Haggie take the easy way home, and for once she actually left without an argument.

"I think that took more out of her than she would like to admit," Mag commented once Hagatha had been dispatched. "Brilliant bit of magic, though."

Clara sighed for what felt like the millionth time that day, "Brilliant, yes, but I don't know if our choice of a memory charm was the best decision."

Mag ignored the comment, her mind having already wandered into figuring out what their next step should be.

Now that it didn't matter if she touched it, she held the golf club aloft and took a couple of practice swings. "Really, anyone who golfs regularly would have had the strength to take someone out with a club like this. It looks like the type they use to drive the ball over long distances."

"It's called a wood. The heads of the clubs used to be made out of hickory, but nowadays they're metal. Lightweight enough to swing, but heavy enough, like you said, to lob the ball a couple of hundred yards down the fairway." Clara supplied.

"Okay, Tiger Woods." Mag raised an inquisitive eyebrow.

"I still have a few secrets of my own, sister dear," Clara retorted. She grabbed the club from Mag's hands, bustled over to the desktop computer that served as a cash register for Balms and Bygones, and began typing furiously.

"It's got the name Sondheim etched into the shaft. Expensive, and made entirely of lightweight titanium. It is, like I said, a fairway wood, and this particular club is part of a set and not commonly sold by itself."

Clara tapped on the keys while Mag watched the screen with a skeptical expression on her face. "This is ludicrous. How is anyone going to have an original thought anymore if they get spoon-fed information just by typing in a question?"

"And you wonder why people always assume you see the glass as half empty. Think about it this way: if you don't have to remember all the small stuff, there's more room in your brain for bigger considerations. If Albert Einstein had a computer to store all the superfluous information rolling around in his head, imagine how much more he could have discovered." Clara enjoyed a moment of silence while her sister contemplated what she'd just said.

"Look." Clara pointed to the screen. "Rolling Hills has a website. A nice one, surprisingly, with links to the pro shop. And guess what? They sell Sondheim clubs. I think it's time for a trip back to the country club. They're going to force us to pay for a membership if we keep showing up there."

"Hey," Mag said, brows raised, "you want to put on one of those little skirts and get rubbed down on a weekly basis, go for it. I'd rather chew leather than spend any more time on closely clipped grass than I have to. Do you know that golf courses are a serious threat to the fresh water supply? Not to mention, all the pesticides they use to make sure their snobby clients don't actually have to come into contact with anything resembling nature."

Mag shook her head. "You're as bad as Hagatha, with her crusade against the mosquitoes and black flies. Why don't you just whip out that blasted cellular phone of yours and call, instead of wasting gas driving all the way over there." She mumbled something unintelligible and unexpected about carbon footprints.

Clara duly ignored Mag's rant, particularly since her sister had made some good points. "The bus runs on magic, as you well know. It doesn't even have an engine, but okay."

After a brief conversation with a woman who, Clara could only assume, was probably another of the brunette clones, she hung up the phone and turned back to Mag. "There's good news and bad news. Which do you want first?"

"Depends on whether you're about to gloat about something."

"I hardly think it's gloating to say I'm right when I'm right." Clara shot back. "The Sondheim titanium 1-wood is sold at the pro shop as part of a twelve-piece set, but you can't get a replacement on site. It gets lost or broken, and you're stuck waiting two weeks for a special order."

"And the bad news?"

"The bad news is, it's their best seller, and half the country club owns a set. Figuring out who owned this one is going to be a challenge." Clara shook her head.

"We could always—" Mag waggled fingers to indicate working magic, "take a peek into the pro shop receipts."

"No. No more breaking and entering. The murderer happened upon Taylor, and presumably had some sort of confrontation, killed him, and then put the club back in the golf bag and drove away. At some point over the last two weeks, he or she caught wind of our involvement and left the club here to cast shade on us." Restless, Clara walked over and mimed putting the club into the umbrella stand.

"Or," she continued, "they figured this would be a great place to get rid of evidence, considering we specialize in used wares. It had to have been during business hours, so one of us has had contact with the murderer. Unfortunately, it could have been just about anyone."

Mag and Clara both searched their memories for anyone suspicious, or anyone who lingered near the umbrella stand, but came up blank. "Maybe Pye or Jinx saw something. They've been manning the store while we've been out on deliveries or investigating."

With worry etching grooves alongside her mouth, Clara called for Pyewacket.

"Can't a cat catch a nap around here?" The warmth pumping off her skin suggested the familiar had been curled up in her favorites spot on the fireplace hearth. "This was supposed to be my day off."

Sloe-eyed and sleepy, she arched her back in that sinuous way cats do.

"I know, dear. But this is important." Clara pointed to the murder weapon. "Have you seen this before? Did someone come in with it?"

Something of the gravity of the situation appeared to reach Pye's sleep-addled brain, and her eyes widened. "I don't think so. Maybe Jinx would know. I'll get him."

In a blur of tawny fur, Pyewacket turned into the cat she was and sped toward the stairs. Moments later she returned alone. "He's not there."

Mag grumbled as she stomped out toward the backyard where she knew Jinx enjoyed sunning himself on a stretch of warm cedar planking that divided Clara's gardens into manageable sections. She caught sight of his fluffy white tail as it flicked with each shake of his hind end.

When he dove into the grass at top speed, Mag assumed he had a field mouse in his sights, but when he trotted back in her direction, she realized he'd been playing with a scrap of crocheted yarn.

"Where did you get that?" she demanded. "If Clara finds out you've ruined one of her projects, she's going to make you eat kitty kibble for a week."

Jinx winked back into human form, spit out the piece of red, yellow, and black striped crochet still in his mouth, and glared at Mag. "This came from the golf course. It's not even Clara's. I figured it was fair game."

Mag plucked the drawstring sack from Jinx's paw-like hand and marched back inside with him on her tail. When the four of them were together, she turned to Jinx, "When did you find this at the golf course? The day Taylor Dean died? That's the only time you've been there as far as I know." She passed it to Clara and watched realization dawn on her sister's face.

Jinx looked between Mag and Clara, his nose twitching from the heat of their gazes, "Yes, that day. I found it on the ground by the mail truck. Why, did I do something wrong?"

"Well, considering it's evidence in a murder investigation—evidence that might have helped us before the cops came knocking on our door—it wasn't your finest feline moment," Clara minced no words.

"This is a golf club cozy—and I know exactly where it came from. Crocheting for Charity makes these by the batch and sells them at the club to raise money for— something I can't remember, or maybe no one ever said." Mag explained.

"Now, I need you to both think back very carefully over the last couple of weeks. Whoever murdered our mailman left this golf club in the umbrella stand sometime during business hours. Have either of you seen anything suspicious, or specifically, did you see who did it? Keep in mind that we've had to take steps to stop the cops breathing down our necks, so please try hard to remember."

Pyewacket shrugged since she'd already answered the question and daintily sniffed the golf club before switching back to cat form and scouring the shop.

Jinx's already pale skin lost another shade, making his eyes stand out bluer than ever. "I don't remember seeing anyone carrying anything that looked like that, but it's busy in here sometimes." Eager to help, he mimicked Pye's thorough sniffing of the club before joining her in the whatever it was the two of them were doing.

After a few minutes only briefly interrupted by the spotting of—and furious attempt to kill—a particularly large dust bunny, the familiars returned to human form and reported to their masters.

"Based on the scent coming off the grip of this club, I'd say it was a woman. I'm getting hand cream—cheap, full of chemicals, nothing like yours, Clara—and something else. An herb, lavender I think. But it's muddled with all the others, like it's been there for a while."

"And lemongrass," Jinx interrupted, not willing to be upstaged. "I smelled it on that floozy or whatever-you-called-it when I picked it up off the ground that day." He had the decency to look ashamed of himself, and Clara wondered once again whether her sister's familiar had lost his touch.

Once a boon companion to the rogue Raythe hunter, Jinx had spent the last forty-odd years in a tuna coma. And he was developing the waistline to prove it.

"This is the key to it all," Mag declared as she waved the brightly striped cozy in the air. "The only clue we have left, and we need to talk to someone who might have more information."

Quickly, Mag and Clara decided the only person they could trust with their newfound question was Babette Dean, and while Mag sent Pye and Jinx scurrying off with their tails between their legs, Clara called Babette and asked her to stop by as soon as possible.

Babette arrived sooner than expected, and Clara led her out to the gardens where she settled into a chair beside the fire pit where Balefire flickered even though the outside thermometer read near on ninety degrees. Babette said she was always cold because of her anemia and didn't seem to mind the gentle heat emanating from the grate.

"We think we might have found a clue to your husband's murder." Clara spoke gently while Mag passed the golf club cozy to Babette. "Do you have any idea who this belongs to? It looks just like the ones we've been making at crochet group."

Babette examined the cozy, taking careful note of the stitching, and shook her head, "It looks like Maude Prescott's handiwork, but we made dozens of these for last's year's sale."

Under her breath, Mag spat a few curse words that came out sounding like a garbled mess, and muttered something about being back where they started. Again.

"Maude usually mans the sales table at the country club." Babette supplied.

"Do you think she might remember who she sold this particular set to?"

Babette shrugged, "Maybe, I'm not sure. We're not really friends, and I don't know enough about her to be able to say. She's sort of an odd duck, if you know what I mean."

Taking offense, Mag sputtered, "She strikes me as a sharp one, so maybe there's hope. Let's ask her about it at crochet group tomorrow."

Chapter Seventeen

"Clara Balefire! Clara! Clara!"

Jarred out of the dream state by the sound of her name screeching through the house, Clara's heart galloped in her chest and stole her breath.

"What on earth is going on?" It was no use asking Pyewacket because, upon the heels of the first shriek, she'd attempted to jump and arch her back at the same time. Now she was cowering under the shade and peeking through the fringe of a frou-frou lampshade, her tail puffed out to three times its normal size.

"Make it stop," Clara begged no one in particular, and tried to pull her scattered wits together.

Penelope Starr's voice roared out of the balefire at an even higher decibel than before.

"Penelope, is that you? What happened?" Must be important if Penelope thought using the magic flames as a communication device a good idea.

Only the pink beginnings of daylight peeked through the curtains as Clara pressed a hand to her forehead and wished for blessed darkness and peace. But it was not to be.

The next sentence Penelope uttered came out garbled, but the few words Clara could make out shouldn't have come as a surprise. Hagatha. Pixies. Up to something.

It couldn't have been anything else.

"Where is she?" Without paying much attention, Clara pointed vaguely at her closet and snapped her fingers. She felt the change between nighttime and daytime wear just as Penelope confirmed Hagatha's location.

"Dawkin's woods. At the circle. Hurry."

"You can bet your broomstick no one else is rushing over there to help. Glorified babysitters are all we are." While Mag took her time getting ready to go, she gave voice to the sentiments both sisters were feeling.

Pitching her tone to match Penelope's shrillness, Clara mocked, "The coven in Harmony needs the Balefire influence. Strong witches make for strong leaders in these changing times. Come to Harmony; you won't be sorry." She fell back into her own voice, "Utter hogwash."

"What she really meant was, *come to Harmony, do all the dirty work.* I've half a mind to go back to bed. You ask me, Hagatha's got the right of it." Mag agreed, yet she still readied herself for what was to come. Potion bottles, packets of herbs, and crystals went into her pockets while Clara chose her most powerful wand and a handful of charmed items.

"At least she doesn't have access to combustion powder. Romilda said she removed every grain from her place." Grateful for small mercies, Clara knew the worst case scenario was off the table.

Mag, of course, knew it was not.

Ready and armed for battle, Mag and Clara took the fastest route to Dawkin's woods, skimming to a secluded spot behind some bushes near the edge of the circle, or, as Clara called it later, the edge of chaos.

There was just enough time to register a few impressions—acrid smoke smearing humid air, mingled scents of burning rock and overly-sweet tropical flowers—before a band of excited pixies arrowed toward the Balefire sisters.

"Ow!" Tiny hands pinched skin, pulled at hair, and poked with sharp toenails as they drove the witches toward the center of the circle.

"Been expecting the pair of you. Can't do nothing these days without the Balefire sisters coming along to muck up the works." At Hagatha's pronouncement, a hint of her magic rippled over Clara's skin, bringing every hair on her body to tingling attention. This was not good.

"Come on, Haggie. You know we're not a threat. Lay off, would you?" Mag chose to cajole rather than lecture and the level of power dropped from the edge of pain to something closer to an itch. "What's going on?"

Now that she wasn't worried about being turned into a black fly or mosquito and chased by hungry honey pixies, she could see for herself what Hagatha was up to.

In the oasis ringed by towering pines sat a miniature volcano. On its sloped sides, female honey pixies lounged suggestively on beds of Faeland flowers. Heat teased the heady scent of tropical perfumes from the tender petals while male pixies darted into and out of the smoke.

Hagatha had set herself up a pixie mating ritual right there in the coven's sacred circle. It might be the worst thing she had done so far. Or, Mag thought, the coolest.

"Where did she get enough combustion powder to do all this?" Resigned to providing little more than enough containment to keep the entire town from feeling the effects, Clara wanted to put Hagatha's dealer on her list for later.

"Um." Slapping on her best innocent face a beat too late, Mag shrugged.

"You didn't? Honestly, Mag, you're almost as bad as she is."

"Well, I didn't know what she was going to do with it, now did I? And it's too late now; we'll just have to let it all play out. What harm can it do, anyway? Way out here, no one will ever know." The toe of Mag's shoe traced an arc in the layer of ash that coated the coating of pine needles littering the circle.

"No one will know?" Clara's voice went up an octave. "Pixies emit powerful pheromones when they mate. Magically powerful, if you get my drift. If we don't contain this now, half the town will be overcome with lust. There will be orgies in the streets. Don't you ever read?"

"Do 'em some good, won't it?" As usual, Hagatha remained unrepentant. "Especially that Penelope Starr. She's due for a good—"

"Don't say another word. Not one." Before any hideous mental images settled behind Clara's eyes, she pulled out her wand and nodded toward Mag's pockets. "Give me those crystals, and I'll spread them outside the circle."

She traded her best wand with Mag for a handful of rainbow-colored stones. "Take this and be ready on my signal. Lock it down before we end up on the national news." As an afterthought, she dug out the charms from her pocket and handed those over, too.

"There's a taunt-repelling charm in there. Pink, rubberized paper clip. I assume your skills run to duplication and we'll need one for each of us. I'll adapt them to repel the pheromones when I get back. Honestly, Mag. This goes beyond the pale."

The glare she cast at her sister hinted there would be more to come on the subject of giving Hagatha the combustion powder, but Clara jogged off to take care of business first.

"Penelope's not the only one," Mag mumbled while she worked up an incantation to create an isolating dome over the circle. It had to be heat proof but still breathable, able to catch the tiniest iota of magic and render everything inside it invisible to passersby.

Not that there should be passersby, but you never knew. None of the coven would deign to show up since they'd dropped their problems into Balefire hands, washing Hagatha clean from their own. Still, better to be prepared.

Hagatha tossed another grain of combustion powder into the mouth of the volcano, and the resulting explosion sent the pixies into a frenzy. Hormones Mag thought long dead flared to life, and for a fleeting moment, she felt young again. Vital.

Until the sensation ended and age settled into her bones again. She mourned the loss for only a few seconds but filed away the experience to think about later.

Clara felt the effects, but not so keenly that she couldn't ignore the flare of heat or the wave of desire as she dropped a carnelian, the final stone, into place and debated whether to remain inside or outside of the circle.

Outside meant she could go home and crawl back into bed, but it also meant leaving Mag alone in an enchanted space with Hagatha.

Raising her left hand, Clara sent a shower of Balefire-infused witchlight into the air, and without waiting for Mag to activate the spell, began making her way back to the center of the circle.

The ground shook once as the dome touched down, nearly knocking Clara off her feet as she made her way back to Mag's side. With the danger of spreading magical lustiness contained, and the paper clip charms protecting the three witches, there was nothing left but to observe the pixie mating spectacle.

"How long is this going to take?" Through the shifting plumes of smoke, Clara scanned the sky for the sun's position and estimated not more than an hour had passed since her rude awakening.

Today was crochet club day, and she didn't want to miss the chance to speak to Maude about the golf club cozy.

"No idea." Cheerful despite the sweat-inducing temperatures, Hagatha looked as daisy-fresh as a witch of her age could look. She tapped her walker with the palms of both hands, turned it into a deck chair complete with side table and umbrella-laden drink, and settled in for the duration.

"This was not how I planned to spend my day." Watching pixies mate wouldn't have hit Clara's list if it were a thousand pages long. Still, there was nothing left to do, so she set about making herself comfortable by turning a convenient bush into a lounger and a pair of pine branches into a fan.

While Mag followed suit and opened up a conversation with Hagatha about the care and feeding of honey pixies, Clara let herself drift off to continue the dream from which she'd been so rudely awakened.

Sleep didn't come easy, what with Hagatha's occasional use of combustion powder to ramp up the action, and the constant chatter between the old witch and Mag over the stamina and prowess exhibited by the males.

It was a lot like being in the middle of one of those documentaries where the announcer speaks with great portent about the fleeting nature of a species. Once or twice, their voices raised to shouts when a male either managed to get the job done or burned up trying.

Hagatha keened each loss since she'd become attached to her charges over the past few weeks.

All Clara wanted was a breath of fresh air and a get-out-of-the-dome-free card. The heat turned her hair to frizz and drained away her vitality.

Add in the stench of burning rock, the smoke that slipped past her makeshift fans, and the low-level hormone bursts even her charms couldn't fully counteract, and she was nothing but a raw nerve.

Mag had to shake her twice to pull Clara out of a daze when it was time to leave. Wisely, the elder Balefire held back comment when her younger sister kicked away the stones anchoring the dome to the earth. One of her best smoky quartz crystals had just sailed into the woods on the wings of Clara's ire.

"It's late, but if we go straight to town from here, we can still catch the end of crochet group." Daring Mag to argue, Clara made the decision. "Aim for the storage closet in Circle headquarters. No one should be there today. We can take the path from there to the library."

"Shouldn't we get cleaned up first?" Once Mag pointed it out, Clara realized she looked like hell. Almost literally, given the smoke damage.

"If I let you go home, we'll never make it back there in time. Aren't you curious to hear what Maude has to say about that cozy? We're witches; we'll use glamour."

"But isn't that against the rules? Penelope will have a fit." Mag grinned; she didn't give a two-bit tin whistle about Penelope or her rules and enjoyed Clara's current state of rebellion.

"She's tap danced on my goodwill for the last time."

Winking out, the sisters reappeared inside the dark closet, and Clara stepped in a bucket before she had the wit to conjure up a ball of witchfire for light.

"This day just gets better and better." Riding her annoyance, Clara sailed out the door leaving Mag, snickering silently, to follow along behind. Glamour in place along with an anti-stinky spell, they hurried toward the library with fifteen minutes to spare before crochet club broke up for the day.

"Don't think I didn't see you making faces at me, and you have a lot of nerve acting as though I'm the one being unreasonable," Clara ranted as she led Mag outside. "You're supposed to be on my side Maggie, and not only did you encourage Hagatha, you provided her with the means to create that mating ritual. What could you have been thinking?"

"Clara, shush," Mag spied an approaching figure and elbowed her sister in the ribs a little harder than necessary. "The name McCreepy is starting to sound more appropriate by the day since that's how frequently we seem to find the mayor of Harmony skulking around in the shadows."

"Well, hello ladies," he greeted both sisters with friendly smiles, but his eyes were trained on Clara's figure, as usual. At least he had enough manners to refocus with a slight blush at Mag's pointed stare.

"Norm," Clara nodded, her gaze flicking to the library. Her thoughts were singularly fixed on pursuing the murder investigation. It was clear Norm McCreery sincerely wished they were focused on pursuing a different sort of satisfaction.

The mayor's grin widened while Clara's faltered at his next statement, "I'm not sure how you did it, but mysteriously, Chief Cobb has declared that the two of you are no longer suspects in Taylor's death."

"Well, that's a relief," Mag commented, maintaining the facade of having no idea what he was talking about.

"In fact, he seems to have forgotten that he questioned your involvement in the first place. Gone right out of his head. Mysterious, that."

Clara flashed him a dazzling smile and brushed off the insinuation. "I'm sure he simply realized he was barking up the wrong tree." She infused her next breath with the faintest hint of magic and leaned a little closer. "You might encourage him to look into Reggie Blackthorne's accounts, once this murder business has been laid to rest."

"Reggie Blackthorne's accounts … yes, those do bear some attention." Mayor McCreery bid the Balefires goodbye and wandered off, shaking his head as if coming out of a daze.

Unfortunately, by the time they reached the darkened doors of the library, knitting group had dispersed, and the opportunity to speak to Maude had passed.

Chapter Eighteen

Parched and filthy under the thin guise of glamour, Clara figured she had about one good burst of magic left in her. She dragged Mag into the dim recesses between the library wall and a bank of shrubbery and winked them both into the middle of her living room.

"I could drink a gallon of water and still not be able to work up a mouthful of spit." While magic runs through the blood of a witch, it also requires a solid connection to all the elements, water being an essential one.

"There's lemonade in my fridge. More Electrolytes. I'll get it." Clara's knees wobbled a bit but carried her there.

"Electowhatsits?" Mag's brow furrowed.

"Lytes. Electrolytes. They're … oh, never mind, just drink it." The pitcher and two glasses landed on the coffee table. "Turn on the ceiling fan, would you? Blow some of the stink off us."

"You look like you took a visit to the sun," Mag figured she probably didn't look much better as the sugar-laced nectar hit her belly. Two glasses later, she announced, "I'm starving."

"There must be something in the fridge, so knock yourself out. I'll be in the shower."

Mag had been right, Clara decided when she caught a glimpse of herself in the mirror. Dusky red tinted all but the skin around her eyes, leaving her to resemble a reverse raccoon. Ten minutes with the taps on cold cooled Clara's bones and took the color down to something between cooked lobster and her normal skin tone.

"My turn." Sprawled across the sofa with her feet propped up on the coffee table, Mag pointed to the plate resting on her belly. "That pear thing was delicious. Almost as good as ice cream. You've been holding out on me."

"What pear thing?"

"Kind of like a tart, or maybe a cake. How should I know? You're the baker." Finally stirring, Mag set the plate on the table, creaked to her feet, and shuffled off into the bathroom leaving Clara staring after her.

Heat stroke must have addled her brains, Clara decided. But when she picked up Mag's plate to put in in the sink, pastry crumbs dotted the pale green surface.

Frowning, Clara yanked open the fridge door and there on the shelf, in an unfamiliar serving plate, she found what Mag had been eating.

The pastry was light golden in the center, with crispy, caramelized edges and studded with slices of glazed and nutmeg-flecked pears. The faintest perfume of lavender tickled Clara's sensitive nose. A tentative forkful proved it tasted as good as it looked.

After a sigh and a second bite, Clara descended the stairs to the shop. "Pye, where did that pear tart come from?"

"It's a galette. One of your customers dropped it off this afternoon. The tall one, with the sour face when she thinks no one is looking. Mavis, something? No, that's not it. Starts with M, though."

"Maude Prescott."

"I guess so." A shiver rippled across Pye's skin. "What happened to you? You're looking a little pink." With no customers in the shop, Pyewacket allowed herself a feline moment. Tawny fur replaced golden skin as she nestled herself into Clara's arms for a cuddle and a chin scratch that soothed both witch and familiar.

"Hagatha." There was no need to say more, and when Mag's footsteps sounded above, Clara reluctantly left Pye to watch the shop.

"Want one?" Caught in the act of cutting a second slice of the galette, Mag offered, but Clara's mind was too busy to answer. Some niggling realization kept poking at the edge of conscious thought and then retreating to tingle along the back of her neck.

A connection between Maude and the pear galette.

"Maude made it." Maybe Mag would pick up the thread. "She dropped it off while we were out."

"I, for one, am not complaining. I'm tasting hints of lavender and nutmeg, but the pears are what makes it special. The texture is silky, smooth. Almost buttery. Sweet, but tender and so juicy. I've never had better."

"Wait a minute." Mag's description sounded like something right out of an advertisement. Because it was. The ad for the fruit of the month club. Racing to her computer, Clara tapped the keys while Mag, plate in hand, watched over her shoulder.

"Look at that, would you?" Scrolling down, Clara read, "Tosca pears, a summer pear from Italy with a silky texture. Featured in this month's club order."

"Well hurrah for Hollywood, but I'm not getting why you're all excited. Now that I'm getting a taste of them, I'm annoyed ours didn't come. But, I'm glad Maude's did."

When it hit her, Mag stopped chewing. "Oh. I see." Her eyes went wide. "I distinctly remember Maude saying her order never came, either."

"Right? So where did she get these?"

Impossible as it seemed, only one scenario covered all the bases. Maude had stolen a fruit of the month order from the mail truck, and the only time she would have had unfettered access to the contents of his mail truck was around the time of Taylor Dean's murder.

"According to the coroner, we arrived on the scene within minutes of his death. Doesn't leave much of a window of opportunity." Thinking back over the timeline, Clara added, "Maude must have seen the killer. Nothing else for it."

But it was Mag who took it to that next step. "Or she *was* the killer."

"Over what? A box of fruit?"

"Maybe," Clara postulated. "People have killed for less. A pair of shoes, an imagined slight. Just for the fun of it."

The more they rehashed the evidence, the more it fit. Maude had been at the club that day, which gave her plenty of opportunity. It stood to reason if she crocheted club cozies for charity, she might also have made a set for herself.

As to motive, there was no evidence of blackmail, but Maude had made no effort to hide her dislike of the mailman. "What about the golf cart? Remember she said they gave away her favorite one?" Going back over everything, Clara wanted to be certain it all fit.

"Easy enough to grab a different one since they just leave them lying around with the keys in. You know, for all the supposed security, the place is no Fort Knox."

"Let's say I agree with you and Maude whacked the mailman. It couldn't have been premeditated, and that's where we've been slipping up all this time. She must have been out golfing and seen him fooling around in the back of the truck the same way we did when we passed by earlier in the day."

Appetite gone, Mag scraped the rest of her pastry into the trash. "He was probably sorting through the packages for something he could lift and turn into a profit later."

Nodding, Clara said, "And then, along came Maude, and caught him at it. 'Where's my fruit order?' and all that jazz. He'd already skipped the delivery, so it either got damaged, or he gave it to Babette. However it happened, the fruit-box ship had sailed."

Mag took over the narrative, "She's carrying the club with her, or maybe it's in the cart. Either way, she snaps. Whack! Down goes the mailman."

"And then she what? Sees our fruit box and just steals it? That's just cold." Cold enough to give Clara a shiver when a vision of it played out in her head.

"Psychotic is what it is, but it's a theory that covers all the bases. The deed is done, so she gets back in the golf cart and rides away. Show me the photos again. The ones you took of the inside of the truck."

Before she did, Clara uploaded the image folder to her computer. "Bigger screen," she explained when Mag huffed over the extra time it took.

"Look, do you see that? Make it bigger. Right there. And can you lighten it up a bit?" After a few seconds of fiddling around with settings, the area Mag had indicated came into focus.

"Dang, Maggie. You've got eyes like a hawk." Maude's fruit-of-the-month-club box, clearly marked for special handling, had been tossed willy-nilly into the mail truck. Not only was it tipped on its side to show her address label, but he'd piled it over with heavier items crumpling the box, and certainly crushing its contents.

Mag fumed. "I think we have a winner. What boils my cauldron is that she planted the murder weapon in the shop to throw suspicion on me."

When a fit of pique set Mag's blood boiling, telltale spurts of magic sometimes leaked out. Like now, when the balefire shot sparks across the room, and the lights flickered. Woebetide Maude Prescott if she could not be brought to justice by other than magical means.

"What are we missing? I feel a sense of foreboding." Never one to ignore witch-based intuition, Clara knew there was a link left unexplored.

She went over the situation again. "For one thing, we have no proof. The murder weapon is a bust, and no one is going to believe she killed a man over a box of pears. Can you imagine the look on Cobb's face if we went in there and accused her? She's in a position to deny everything and get away with murder." Maude's eternal fate edged closer to being circumvented by magical means.

"I could turn her into a worm and let her loose in a pear grove as a bit of divine retribution." Mag wouldn't hesitate.

Clara directed a quelling look in her sister's direction and asked her to go over the conversation from the last crochet group again. "How did she figure out you were on the suspect list?"

"It wasn't difficult, Clarie. She was here the day Cobb came around asking questions, and then the club turned up here."

"That's why she was out of breath when I went outside after he left. Hotfooting it away so I wouldn't catch her eavesdropping." When Clara played it back it seemed so obvious.

Meg scowled, irritated because she'd just started to like the woman. "You didn't tell me about that. Probably didn't seem important, because who would suspect Maude? If she tells Babette the cozy was hers, though, then I think we've got her."

Babette.

At the mention of her name, tension seized control of Clara's spine. If this theory proved correct, they'd sent Babette into the den of a killer with the only piece of evidence that mattered: the golf club cozy.

Clara called Babette, her heart sinking more with each unanswered ring. Meeting Mag's questioning gaze, Clara shook her head. "She's not picking up."

"I'll drive." Time wasted on arguing was time Babette might not have, so with Mag behind the wheel, Clara worked on their excuse for dropping by unexpectedly.

Conjuring up a box of supplies, she visualized a dozen finished golf club cozies. Variegated yarn slid and knotted over steel hooks while Clara orchestrated with flashing fingers. The last one, an exact match to the one Jinx had found at the scene of the crime, knotted itself securely and fell into the box as Mag screeched the bus to a halt.

"You schmooze, I'll snoop. It's best to play to our strengths."

Feeling a little like the fly, Clara rang the bell and waited for the spider to invite them into her web.

"Why, Clara. What a lovely surprise." Now that they knew to look, it was easy to see the lie behind her Maude's eyes. She was not happy to have visitors. Not one bit. But, as manners dictated, she led Clara inside, where the foyer opened into a small-scale but enviable chef's kitchen.

"I missed you at crochet group. Unavoidably detained, don't you know, and I wanted to get these to you today." Shooting for affable, and folksy in her tone, Clara set her sights on distracting Maude long enough for Mag to work whatever mojo she had in mind.

If Penelope Starr wanted to argue over magic used to save a life, she'd be dealing with both Balefire sisters for a change.

"Could you take a look at my work? These are my first attempts, and I'm not sure if they're up to par." With a grin that didn't quite make it up to her eyes, Clara tossed in the pun and opened up the box.

If there had been any more need for proof, Maude removed it by snatching up the replica cozy and seizing Clara by the arm. "Where did you get this?"

"I told you, I made these for the sale. Is something wrong?"

With Maude's attention focused on Clara, Mag activated the silencing charm she carried in her pocket and took a step around Maude and moved toward the back of the house.

An audible step.

She'd neglected to cleanse the charm under running water after its third use. Just great.

"You made this? This pattern? These colors?" Face a dull red, eyes blazing, Maude's attention was so focused on Clara, Mag could have done the hokey pokey without being noticed, so she hurried from the room.

"I'm sorry, I don't know what I did wrong." So much for schmoozing, Clara thought and rolled with the changes. "I saw the combination somewhere and I liked it. I had no idea you'd be so upset. Tell me what's wrong, Maude. I didn't mean to cause offense."

Under the dithering front, Clara's resolve turned to steel. Drawing on the fire that brought her magic to life, Clara turned up the heat until the vice-like grip on her arm fell away.

"No, I'm the one who's sorry. I had a set just like these, and one turned up missing."

"What a shame." Clara needed to buy Mag more time. "By the way, that pear tart was fabulous. The lavender came through just perfectly. Top-notch bake and the pears were delectable. They were Tosca pears?"

"They were, indeed. The featured item in the club this month."

Clara's eyes narrowed, and suddenly, she appeared less like an unwelcome nuisance and more like a formidable opponent, "I wouldn't know because I never received my fruit basket. Any idea why?"

Maude blanched and stared at Clara for a moment before realizing that her secret wasn't one any longer. When Maude looked frantically around, her eyes lighting on a sizable carving knife lying on the counter, Clara understood that Maude knew she'd been discovered.

Clara felt adrenaline course through her veins and, taking advantage of nature's danger indicator, combined the rush with a swell of magic. Hagatha's magic, to be precise. Calling on the elements, Clara let her intention flow. Earth, air, fire, and water all ceased activity, turning Maude into a harmless mannequin, poised over her kitchen counter with knife in hand. Minus the ferocious expression on Maude's face, and with the addition of an apron and chef's hat, she could have passed for a television cook.

Leaving Maude frozen in the kitchen, Mag led Clara to Babette's too-still form. "She's been poisoned. I've done what I could to slow the effects. Bought her a few hours, but it's spread too far, and I can't reverse it. We need to get her to a hospital, and even then, it's not looking good."

"There must be something we can do. We dragged her into this, it's up to us to get her out." Looking down at Babette's face, Clara felt her heart breaking. "We have to try."

"We were too late. I'm sorry, Clarie. I don't think there's anything—" Something flipped in Mag's memory banks. "Wait. Let me think a minute."

A recent conversation, the word poison. Mag tried to bring the elusive memory into focus.

Hagatha and the honey pixies.

"You're not going to like this, but I think we need honey."

Brightening with hope, Clara said, "Maude's a baker, I bet there's plenty in her kitchen."

"Pixie honey."

Chapter Nineteen

"I hate to leave her alone like this," but Clara knew Mag was right. A visit to the honey pixies was the only way to save Babette's life, and waiting was no longer an option.

Had it only been a week or two since they'd found Hagatha's haven? She'd been busy in the meantime settling her charm of pixies into their own little Faelands oasis.

"That's—" Mag searched for the word she wanted as she examined the progress.

"Scandalous? A breach of the inter-species compact?"

"—impressive."

"That, too. Is that the hive?"

About the size of a basketball, the hive swung on the end of a multi-strand rope that looked like it had been woven from spiderweb. A delicate confection of a thing, woven from flower petals and studded with insect wings, it fairly glittered in the sunlight.

A pile of polished granite rose through the center of the secluded grove, moss and soil tucked into each cranny and crevice to create planting beds for a kaleidoscope of colorful flowers. Water fountained like a shower of crystals from the peak of the homemade mountain and cascaded down to form a lagoon at the base.

Halfway up, a trickle of water diverted to create a shallow pool—the birthplace of a rainbow. Every so often, a drop of nectar built up on the end of the colorful arch and dripped into a hole at the top of the hive.

Pixies, many more than had attended the mating ritual, lounged and flitted everywhere the sister witches looked. Their chances of sneaking in and stealing a drop or two of honey fell somewhere between zero and none at all.

"Now what?" Clara wondered.

"How should I know?"

"You're the one who spent half the day discussing their mating habits with Hagatha, so you tell me. Maybe they're friendly and we can just—" Clara took a long step toward the hive and a hastier two steps back when an angry buzz smeared the air. "Nope."

"Let me try something." Keeping her feet planted, Mag called out, "Maypole!" And then she waited. Again. "Maypole! Are you here?"

The familiar chirp sounded behind her and Mag whirled to see the pixie hovering at eye level. "Oh, there you are. We need your help. Can you understand me?"

Tilting her head, the tiny pixie seemed to be considering the question. Finally, she nodded.

"We need your help." Mag repeated. "Someone has been hurt badly, and Hagatha told me you produce a serum that makes your honey good for healing."

At the mention of honey, Maypole's little face went hard. She shook her head and clenched her fists for good measure.

"Please, it's important. Someone's life hangs in the balance." Not above begging, Clara pleaded.

"It's no use."

Both witches jumped when Hagatha's voice cracked like a whip. She must have skimmed in from somewhere nearby.

"Maybe you can get them to see reason." As concisely as possible, Clara explained the situation.

"What do you think I've been doing all this for? I figured if I gave them a safe space—you know they've been hunted to near extinction in the Faelands—they'd offer me a drop or two in trade. So far, that's been a bust."

Landing on Hagatha's shoulder, Maypole grasped the rim of her ear, leaned in, and talked a blue streak.

"She says this place is nice, but even safety isn't a good enough trade for their wares. I'd need something they prize more than their own skins."

"And what might that be?" Clara asked, but Mag already had an answer.

She dug into her arsenal and pulled out the bottle containing the Andruvian trumpet flower. "This."

"You've been holding out on me," Hagatha accused and reached for the bottle.

"Not so fast." Mag snatched it away. "I'm prepared to allow each pixie one sip of nectar if they'll let us harvest the honey we need, and I promise not to take advantage. I might have a few things that would help you keep your little rescue operation secret if you'll help us figure out the antidote. Babette's running out of time."

Maypole let out a pixie-sized shriek of excitement. Her little voice fluting, she returned to her charm to deliver the news of their impending good fortune. Titillation flared through the little community, though not every pixie seemed to be on board with the trade.

A dozen or so of the tiny bodies rose into the air, wings buzzing, and arrowed toward Mag. As they flew past, Clara ducked and experienced a flashback to an old horror movie moment, but Mag never even flinched. Guts of steel, that one.

Instead, she popped the top on the potion bottle, and cupped the trumpet flower, wafting it gently to send the scent of nectar toward the attack team.

"Do we have a deal?"

The angry buzz gentled to something closer to a purr.

"Clara, if you and Hagatha could get Maypole to hurry with the honey, I'll just handle this end of things." As soon as the other two witches complied, she added,

"Come on, then, you lot. Gather round, one sip only. I'll be watching you."

In a hot second, Mag found herself covered with feathered creatures with no time to marvel over the experience. When a blush-pink pixie landed on her nose, she heard the distinct sound of Clara's phone capturing a photo, and was, for once, thankful for the infernal device. This was the moment of a lifetime.

Twenty minutes passed—long minutes that marked the march toward the end of Babette's life, but were necessary all the same—before it was Maypole's turn to take the last sip. Leaving a delicate belch behind her, she wobbled into the air and joined her brethren near the lagoon.

"Got it." Clara held up a vial of honey. "Now what, Hagatha?"

"Timeline makes it complicated," the old witch said. "We're past the point where a simple antidote is enough. Needs a strong healing component and then it's still going to be a near thing. I'll do my best, but it might not be good enough."

"What do we need?" Capping the top on the now bedraggled trumpet flower, Mag was all business.

"Gertrude Granger," Hagatha replied. "Christmas spirit isn't easy to find this time of year, but I think it's the only way this is going to work. Two parts honey, one part Christmas spirit, and a drop of the blood of the poisoner added to your basic healing tonic."

"Maude's going to love that one," Clara said. "Good thing she's immobile and can't put up a fight."

"We'll need ritual candles, sage for cleansing. Crystals." All of which Mag had packed in her pockets.

Winking into Gertrude's living room unannounced breached the witch's code of decency, if there were such a thing, but there was no time for being polite.

"Sorry, Gertrude. We hate to barge in like this." Taking the reins, Clara apologized loudly and got right to the point. "But we need your help."

As always, the scent of Christmas cookies perfumed the air. Gertrude should probably buy stock in the cinnamon industry—she probably wouldn't make anything, but it would offset some of her expenses. Unfortunately, she wasn't alone when she rushed out of the kitchen.

"Well, hello Penelope. Didn't expect to run into you here." Mag couldn't bring herself to act as though it was a welcome surprise.

"I should say not." Penelope looked like she wanted to say more, but a glare from Hagatha shut her up. Momentarily, at least.

A glance passed between Mag and Clara, and then a shrug. They'd have to explain the situation and hope Penelope had a wider charitable streak than expected. Besides, there wasn't anything she could do to stop them.

Running the Moonstones gave the uppity witch a lot less control than she'd come to believe, and it might be time for her to learn that lesson. If it was, Mag was happy to act as teacher, so she ignored Penelope and focused on Gertrude.

"We've run into a bit of trouble, and someone needs your help. It's a matter of life and death." Laying out the situation in as few words as possible, Clara kept a firm grip on Hagatha's arm. The old witch's big mouth and her penchant for mischief would add nothing useful to the situation.

"Why should we concern ourselves with the lives of mortals? They're not our responsibility." Penelope's comment came as no great surprise.

"Hypocrite." Shaking off Clara's grip, Hagatha stated her opinion and the tension in the room went up a notch. "Look down your nose at mortals, and try to force your coven to act just like them. I won't have it."

Penelope offered no denial, "I still don't see how this is our problem."

Gertrude's heart was touched.

"Because all life is precious," she reprimanded and then turned to Clara. "Whatever you need, it's yours."

It occurred to Clara that Penelope's immediate dismissal had worked so thoroughly in their favor, it was a blessing she'd been there to shove Gertrude out of terminal wishy-washiness. When Penelope caught her eye and gave the barest hint of a raised eyebrow, Clara wondered what was going on inside the younger witch's head.

Everyone has a story to tell, and Penelope's might be worth a listen.

But not today.

Today was for justice and for saving Babette. And for truth and the American way. Okay, Clara thought, maybe that last bit was over the top, but the rest was spot-on.

Mag handed Gertrude a bottle. "Fill 'er up."

Gertrude nodded. "From my strongest batch." She carried the bottle off to make due on her promise while Penelope eyed Mag defiantly.

"I'm going with you," she said.

"Knock yourself out, but if you try to stop us helping Babette Dean, I'll let Hagatha have her way with you," Mag warned.

"Oh, you'd like that. She'd kill me and end up stoned, so you could take over the coven."

As conspiracy theories went, it wasn't the oddest Mag had ever heard, but certainly, the furthest from the truth and, surprisingly, Penelope's vehemence tickled her funny bone.

"Is that what you think we're after?" Mag hooted. "You all came to us, remember. Begging the Balefire witches to come here and clean up after—"

Oops, she'd almost mentioned the Hagatha situation right in front of the old witch herself.

"Please," Haggie snorted. "I'm not senile, and we don't have time for stroking egos. Here comes Gertrude with the goods."

The glimmer and shine of the essence she carried cast red and gold light over her face. "Santa will be so pleased. I'm sure to move to the top of his list."

"Her tree isn't lighted all the way to the top, is it?" Hagatha whispered in Mag's ear.

There was no holding back the snort, and Mag figured it would give her indigestion if she tried. "No, probably not."

Armed with the spirit of hope and a jar of magical honey, and with Mag leading the way, the five witches skimmed through space to land in Maude's kitchen.

Chapter Twenty

Breezing past an immobile Maude, the witches tumbled into the back bedroom where Babette rested on a brass-framed bed covered in a frilly, pale pink duvet. Without a word, the women who represented roughly a third of the Harmony coven worked together seamlessly, much to their surprise.

"We'll be exposed, but I suppose it can't be helped." Gertrude flicked the bed into the center of the room with a wave of her wand, and Penelope pulled a jar of salt from the depths of her purse and sprinkled a ring around it.

Clara and Hagatha called to the elemental spirits— the Goddesses of earth, air, fire, and water—to create a protective cocoon of healing energy.

"Good thinking." Mag gave the thumbs up. "Every little bit helps."

With the pieces in place, it was time to administer the remedy, and Mag was the one who poured the contents of the vial unceremoniously down Babette's throat. Then it was Hagatha's turn to supply the final bit of magic that would pull the whole ritual together.

Arms stretched out to her sides, Hagatha channeled power from the four corners, from the elements, from the other witches, and from Babette, herself. So strong was the force, it lit her from the inside out.

A barely perceptible nod of her head sent the covers flying into a corner. Lightning sizzled and sparked across the distance between the old witch's hands and Babette's body. Inch by inch, from head to toe, Hagatha cleansed blood, and bone, and sinew, but still her fingers searched for more.

Ripples flowed beneath pale skin as the potion traveled, gathering poison and sickness until Hagatha let out a sharp sound. Her head tipped skyward as she pulled out a ball of seething darkness and held it aloft.

"I need to …" Hagatha's glance darted around the room until she found what she needed. She lurched across the room to plunge the ball into the earth sheltering the roots of a potted Schefflera that withered and died in a sort of slow-motion reverse.

"Shame," she said, "to ruin a perfectly good umbrella tree like that, but what are you going to do? I wasn't expecting anything quite that big when you said a single dose of poison."

"As far as we knew, it was a small dose, but Babette had a delicate constitution," Clara explained.

"Not anymore." Hagatha grinned as Babette stirred and put a hand to her head.

"What happened? Where am I? What are you doing here?" Voice scratchy but gaining strength, Babette tried to orient herself to time and place.

"You're at—" Clara laid a hand on Babette's arm, gave it a squeeze.

"Maude Prescott tried to kill me." Remembering, Babette bolted upright. "When I came to ask her about that club cozy, she invited me in and offered me tea. It's a little hazy, but I remember her telling me she was sorry, but it was time for me to join my Taylor. I think she killed him and then tried to kill me."

Her story confirmed what Mag and Clara had already figured out.

"I have to do something, stop her before she gets away." Shrugging off Clara's hand, she made to rise.

"Stop." Mag's voice carried such authority Babette froze. "Let us handle Maude while you get your strength back. I promise we won't let her get away. Penelope, if you'd be so kind, please sit with Mrs. Dean a minute more."

Left with little choice, Penelope complied.

Hagatha marched right up to Maude, and Clara wondered for a second if she intended to inflict bodily harm. But the old witch just walked around with narrowed eyes, peering into Maude's face for a long moment before fixing her gaze on Clara. "Impressive bit of spell work, if I may say. Wasn't sure you had it in you. Immobilizing a target like that takes a lot of practice."

Clara blushed and quickly risked a look at her sister's face. Admiration mixed with a tinge of sadness peered back at her. "It was my first time. I'm not even sure how I did it. Adrenaline, I think."

Accepting praise didn't come easily to Clara, so she quickly changed the subject. "Now, what are we going to do about her?"

"Turn her over to the police, and let them deal with her?" Gertrude suggested.

"We can't just unfreeze her, and I, for one, want to hear what she has to say for herself," Mag interjected. "After all, the woman tried to frame me for murder, and when we restore her, she's going to have an interesting story to tell. At the very least, we've got to wipe her memory. Clarie, can you undo the spell?"

Clara exchanged a look with Hagatha, who nodded once toward Maude. "You can do it, and she's not going anywhere. I'll see to that."

For a moment, Clara stood as still as stone—not an entirely new look for her—and concentrated while Mag, Hagatha, and Gertrude blocked the exits in case Maude tried to bolt. She angled her wand toward the murderous woman and spoke an incantation infused with the most important tool a witch has at her disposal: intention.

Maude returned to the land of the living as if no time had passed, still reaching toward the knife she'd intended for Clara.

"Don't even think about it." Hagatha spoke without inflection or heat, which made the order all the more chilling. Maude's hand dropped, and so did her lower jaw.

"The jig is up, Maude Prescott," Mag thundered. "We know what you did, so you might as well confess."

"If you think I'm going to go gently into *that* good night, you're wrong. I only did what I had to do, and the evidence against me is circumstantial at best." Maude crossed her arms and zipped her lips.

Babette picked the perfect moment to make her grand entrance, which she did with Penelope on her heels. "Not if you include my statement that you poisoned me. I don't know what these women did, but I feel right as rain now, and I'm ready to hear you talk. Why did you take my husband away from me? What did I ever do to you?"

Emotion swirled behind Maude's eyes, flickering from shock at seeing Babette alive and well, through anger and fear, finally settling somewhere between resignation and an iota of remorse.

"I didn't intend to hurt anyone." She sighed and slid onto one of the tall stools lined up next to the kitchen island, and dropped her head into her hands.

"I had just finished a round of golf and decided to do a lap in the cart before returning it. The breeze through my hair felt so nice, and I had the pear galette recipe on my mind. When I saw Taylor's truck, I thought it was serendipity. I just wanted my fruit-of-the-month basket, but when I got closer, I realized what he was doing. Tampering with the mail, he was."

Her breath hitched, then her voice raised an octave, and she waved her hand, angry. "And there was my fruit-of-the-month-club box, crushed half flat. My Tosca pears, ruined. He truly was the worst mailman on the planet."

If that was her excuse, it was a flimsy one.

"White-hot rage rolled through me as I walked back to the cart. I don't know what happened, honestly, but I knew I needed to do something. I grabbed the club and did the world a favor." To Babette, she said, "I'm sorry, dear, but you're better off."

Turning to Mag, Maude admitted, "I took your box of fruit. It was the wrong thing to do. I made you a nice galette, though."

As if that was her biggest crime.

"You're crazy. You're going to spend the rest of your life behind bars," Clara said.

"Positively psychopathic," Mag agreed.

"I never noticed I was missing one of my golf club cozies until I heard the police accuse one of the Balefires, and it occurred to me she'd make the perfect patsy. Leaving the club at your shop should have worked, but then Babette showed up here, and I knew I needed to get rid of her, too."

She pointed toward a plastic water bottle sitting open on the counter near her hand. "You should be dead. Why aren't you dead?"

Maude's shoulders squared resolutely, and before anyone had time to make a move, she grabbed the bottle of poison and swallowed what was left. Her eyes widened, then went blank, and she slumped, unconscious to the floor.

"No!" Clara yelled, rushing to Maude's side. She attempted CPR and was about to throw caution to the wind and call upon the magics when Hagatha interrupted her ministrations.

"It's too late. This is what she wanted. Let her go."

In death, Maude's face lost the severe look lent by a self-righteous personality and the constraints of living up to her own ideals. Sadly, Clara thought there had been a kind of unexpected beauty underneath.

"I'll call 9-1-1." Babette volunteered, her face an unreadable mask.

Hagatha and Gertrude were the first to give Deputy Nye their statements when the young officer arrived on the scene a scant fifteen minutes later.

Gertrude offered to skim Hagatha home, which sparked a short argument and some harsh words from old Haggie about being thought feeble-bodied. In the end, they settled on the long route and toddled off together with Gertrude talking a blue streak all the way down the block.

Penelope hung back until the coroner had loaded Maude's body and the rear lights of the ambulance disappeared into the night. "Can I have a word, please?"

Mag and Clara exchanged a rueful eye roll; they'd expected backlash and settled in for the duration.

For once, Penelope Starr's expression lacked the usual measure of disdain as she directed her words to Clara. "It's possible I may have slightly misjudged your character."

Mag snorted, considering the use of the word 'slightly' as just slightly insulting.

"You wanted to save Maude's life back there. Even though, it would seem, she didn't deserve it. I have to say, your actions didn't jive with my perception of you as a murderous witch."

Exasperated and protective, Mag answered for her sister, "That's because you've been incapable of listening to reason. We've tried to explain how Clara ended up encased in stone—as much of it as she's willing to share, considering it's private, anyway. Had she killed her own daughter, she'd still be a statue. Sylvana is alive and well, and that's all the proof you should have needed."

Clara rested a hand on Mag's arm, "Penelope, I accept your *apology*." She assumed that the admission of error was as close as Penelope could come to one, but still emphasized the word. "I don't expect us to become best friends, but we are part of the same coven, and I am willing to try to get along."

Her voice held a level of gentle reproach. "Which means you've got to ease up on some of these rules. We're going to need all the power at our disposal if we're going to continue to keep Hagatha's exploits under wraps. Annoying the pants off the rest of us seems to have become an obsession. We'll handle it, but you have to back off. Agreed?"

Lynn Nye unrolled the yellow tape, prepared to fasten it over the door, and gave the Balefire sisters a pointed look that said she was finished with them for now.

Taking the hint, they prepared to leave.

"You know, Maggie, I could have killed you when I found out you'd given Hagatha that combustion powder. But, if you hadn't, we might not have had what we needed to save Babette. Her death would be on my hands, and I'm not sure I could have handled it."

Mag's response came in the form of an elbow nudge.

"I'm serious. What I'm trying to say is, I'm sorry I gave you such a hard time, and I'm glad to have you around." Clara's sentiment was sincere, and Mag cracked a rare, genuine grin.

"No problem, sis. I'll continue to be a pain in your badonkadonk for as long as you'll let me." Mag quipped.

"Also," Clara hedged, wandering into dangerous emotional territory, "I have to know. What was on your mind when Hagatha was complimenting me in the kitchen? About the immobility spell on Maude."

Mag was silent for a long moment, and Clara swore she saw a tear welling in the corner of her sister's eye. "A moment of self-pity. And before you start feeling bad, let me just say that I'm extremely proud of you for having pulled it off. I can manage small things, like insects and the rare squirrel or rabbit, but a human is an entirely 'nother level. Not as difficult as demons, though. Or hell beasts. They're fast. Much too fast."

Realization dawned on Clara, and she reached for Mag's hand, gave it a comforting squeeze while allowing the revelation to continue uninterrupted.

"That's the second time you've shown me a skill that could have prevented this," Mag indicated her aged appearance. "You have no idea how invaluable your little soda-can-tab-silencing charm would have been to me during my hunting days. It seems I might have a thing or two to learn from my little sister."

Clara glowed under the praise of the person she'd spent more than a human lifetime trying to impress. "Seems like we work best as a team." She was about to suggest she and Mag should stick together when a pink, bee-sized body zipped toward her face.

The baby pixie hovered at nose height long enough for Clara to get a good look at it's cherubic face. Adorable. And trouble, she knew just be looking.

When a second, harried-looking pixie winged close, the baby chirped once, and fled.

"Did Hagatha happen mention anything about the duration of a pixie's gestation period?" Clara asked Mag.

"No, but I'm assuming it's not lengthy. And you're going to have fun coming up with a good story to tell Angela and the garden club." Smug, Mag grinned." But for now, I think it's time for some butter pecan ice cream."

The End